TOCABAGA 7

Pàn Guó Zuì

叛国罪

HIGH TREASON

THOMAS H. WARD

TOCABAGA 7:

Pàn Guó Zuì

叛国罪

HIGH TREASON

by

THOMAS H. WARD

ISBN-13: 978-0692337868

ISBN-10: 0692337865

Transcendent Publishing
www.transcendentpublishing.com

SYNOPSIS

What does the future hold for America? Read "The Tocabaga Chronicles" to find out what could happen to our wonderful country. Find out how to protect your loved ones and survive the chaos after the collapse.

Law and order only exists at the end of a gun. It takes tough, hard men and women working as a team to stay safe and free. Friends and family need to stick together to fend off the daily threats of death. You need to be smart, compassionate, and ruthless with those who would do you harm. You need guns, guns, and more guns with a ton of ammunition or you will not survive very long.

Good luck in the future.

THOMAS H. WARD

PROLUGE

I see them all the time. I see them walking around the streets when I drive by vacant run down homes where people used to live normal lives. They're the poor, the homeless, the starving, and the mentally ill who have no future. The homeless wander aimlessly around not knowing where they are going or where they have been. They are all searching for the same things: which are food and safe shelter. In reality they have no hope to improve their lives. These people have nothing, no money, no food, and no home. They wear dirty rags for clothes and live in fear every day. People are forced to sleep in dirty rat-invested, termite riddled, old homes or buildings. Most will die on the streets from starvation or malnutrition if they aren't murdered first by the Free Roamers for the rags on their backs. The Free Roamers are small groups of people who roam around stealing from the weak and sick helpless people.

Now we are a third world country like Mexico, India, and China. These countries and others have thousands of poor people trying to stay alive. They don't know where their next meal will come from.

In Mexico, years ago, there was a shanty town just south of Tijuana on the main highway. It had thousands of houses made of cardboard and plywood located on the side of a large hill. These so-called houses had no running water or toilets. Driving by you could see little kids playing in the mud or maybe it wasn't mud. You could smell the stench from the highway hundreds of yards away. It was the smell of garbage and human waste that was so strong you needed to hold your nose or puke in your own car.

Mexicali, along the border of California, was a sleepy little town. It looked like something out of a western movie. A mud and dirt street ran through the middle of town. The wooden sidewalks, were raised up about two feet off the ground and followed the store fronts. There were even hitching posts where one could tie up a horse. This small town was under the thumb of drug cartels. Every man you saw carried a side arm of some kind. Going through town was dangerous but not because of the cartel. It was dangerous because of the kids who would approach your car at a stop light and clean your windows. They were starving drug addicted little kids.

Mexicali had a stop light on every corner. You had to stop because if a cop saw you run a light you could go jail or be forced pay a big fine. When you stopped for a red light the little drug kids would come up to your car and clean your windows. When they finished they wanted you to pay them. If you rolled down your window to give them money, one would stick a gun in your face and take all your money. The only way to prevent this was to brandish your own gun. Once they saw you were armed they would leave you alone. These poor kids were making money the only way they knew how. They needed to buy food and the drugs that the cartel got them hooked on.

One time in India I stayed at a four-star hotel in Bombay. I had a well-off friend that owned an electronics company. I went for a walk to see the city the day I arrived. Near the front door of the hotel, on the sidewalk, lay a dead man. Everyone was stepping over or around him. I went back inside and told the front desk about the dead body. They told me not to worry because someone will come by to pick up it up soon. I went for my walk and before I knew it little kids were swarming all around me. They were touching me all over trying to pick my pockets. A dozen little kids dressed in rags with dirty hungry faces. These kids, I found out later, are called the untouchables. They are the poorest of the poor, all of them slowly starving to death, looking for money. To keep them from touching me, and passing on some type of disease, I took all the money in my pockets and threw it up in the air. They all scrambled for it while I made my escape. My Indian friend told me not to go walking around because those kids would kill you for a dollar.

I never thought the United States of America would become a third world country. It makes me sick to think about it. I feel sorry for most of these helpless American kids. I would bring them all to Tocabaga, if I could, but that would overwhelm our food supply and create a dangerous situation for Tocabaga citizens.

I try to look the other way and not become involved, but every now and then something compels me to stop and talk to these people. Maybe it's God telling me to help them. I stop especially if I see a kid or a family with kids in need.

I talk to them and determine if they are of good moral character or worth saving. I know I am playing God, in a way, deciding who will live and die. If they are worth saving I bring them to Tocabaga. This upsets a lot of people here and causes problems. Our population has increased by fifty people in the last few months. The Tocabaga

Board warned me not to bring any more refugees to our sanctuary because it is stressful for those already here and it puts a strain on our resources.

The problem is if I see any little kids walking the streets by themselves I have to help them. The only way to help them is to take them off the streets and bring them here so they can have a, more or less, normal life.

We need these kids because they are the future. They're the ones who will keep the dream alive. They're the ones that will grow our food and do our chores when we are too old to take care of ourselves.

I have adopted four children, bringing my extended family to a total of twelve people. Other citizens have taken in at least a dozen more children. These children are learning about the Constitution and our history. We are teaching them how to farm and hunt to become self sufficient. They're learning how to take care of others and show compassion. They're learning how to fight for freedom.

How did our country get this way? My thinking is it was a number of things, but it was also an overzealous President who was pushing for more control of the government to make a truly socialist state.

The country was overwhelmed by illegal aliens coming across our unprotected borders.

These people wanted what we had worked for all our lives. They wanted us to give them food and homes or they would take it by force.

Soon the number of people not paying taxes overwhelmed the system by wanting more and more free services. The government couldn't afford it anymore and everything just fell apart.

China now holds 46 percent of all U.S. debt. It is the largest holder of all U.S. debt. If the United States cannot repay the debt in an international currency or gold then China could demand payment in tangible property, such as real estate.

If you check history, many lands were sold or given as payment of debt. The United States took over Texas, California, Arizona, and New Mexico after the Mexican-American War as payment. We purchased Alaska from Russia. The U.S. purchased land from France in a deal called the Louisiana Purchase. Spain ceded Florida to the United States in 1821.

The current President put into effect Executive Order 13603 which declared that all property belongs to the Federal Government: your house, money, guns, and even your kids. They can tell you where to live and where to work. If you don't think this can happen then Google U. S. internment camps.

In 1942 President Roosevelt issued Executive Order 9066 which put over 120,000

Japanese Americans in camps taking away their freedom and Constitutional rights. This is fact that many Americans don't know about. German Americans were also put into camps. The Presidential Order was given because these Americans were deemed a threat by the government. The President has a lot of power and can become a dictator if inclined to do so.

The Military is split over whether to follow the President's orders which violate the US Constitution or to support the people. The regular Army is standing down but the Special Forces which include the Army Rangers, Delta Force, Airborne troops, Navy Seals, and other special operations have taken the side of the people and the Constitution. It's a civil war over the rights' of the people versus the government.

Years before, things weren't making much sense especially when the government took control of the news media. It became state-owned so the only news we received was what the Federal Government wanted us to hear. Back in 2013 the NSA started to tap our phones, read our emails, and Facebook pages. We were all being watched, we were all suspected of doing something wrong. We were having our Bill of Rights violated in the name of government security, and no one did anything about it.

Benjamin Franklin once said, "He who

sacrifices freedom for security deserves neither."

Unemployment shot up to 55% and everyone knew that things were changing as more and more acts of violence were reported across the nation. Riots, robberies, shootings, explosions, and even attacks on police stations were common. Some states called up the National Guard to help maintain control since desperate people can do desperate things. The National Guard didn't help. It fell into disarray. Just driving to the grocery store was dangerous. You needed to carry a gun for safety or your trip to the store could end up being your last.

Our currency became worthless due to inflation and the government closed all the banks to stop bank runs. A loaf of bread rose to $100 and milk to $150 per gallon. People ran out of money and even if they had any in the bank, they couldn't take it out. The banks were closed. Savings accounts were wiped out and if you had any gold or silver in the bank, you were out of luck. The government took it because the country is bankrupt.

For many years illegal aliens have been coming across the border from Mexico. But not all the people are hardworking Mexicans looking for work. The fact is many of those crossing the border are from the Middle East and are related to Islamic radical terrorist groups.

The gangs and cartels that smuggle dope are also making inroads into the US selling their crap to whatever idiots will buy it. These gangs have turf wars and during their wars they don't care whom they kill. Then there are the drug users who rob and kill to obtain money to pay for their habit. Finally, we have the radical groups like the Skinheads, Neo-Nazis, some extremely violent religious people, and those that want white supremacy.

There are food lines at government controlled stores. You must wait for hours to get any food. If you can buy any food it is only enough for a few days. You can't feed your family on a loaf of bread. Fresh vegetables and fruit cannot be found. Everything is canned goods or freeze dried ready to eat meals.

The question is, can we change what we have become? There is no country to help us as they have all failed. We are the last hope of free mankind. We can't forget the Bill of Rights, the United States Constitution, and the fact we are One Nation under God.

Here on Tocabaga we grow all our own food in a Forty-acre garden. We found that we could grow almost any type of vegetable or fruit. Tocabaga has a chicken farm that provides eggs and chickens to our group. Most of our protein comes from eating fish. We have forty people that fish everyday to provide about 500 pounds a day to feed our group. There are crabs, clams, and oysters that we harvest most of the year. We also hunt wild pigs, deer, birds, and rabbits for protein.

Everyone on Tocabaga works or has a job function to perform. If you don't work you don't eat. We have farmers, fishing crews, cooks, and lawn crews to fight back the fast growing jungle. We have auto mechanics and repairmen that can fix anything that breaks down. Most important of all we have trained security people along with twenty Amazon Warriors who act as our police force. Everyone knows their job but each group has a lead man or supervisor that directs daily activities. The supervisors meet once a week to coordinate activities for the whole island.

We have a Board of Directors made up of 12 members who have been elected by the people living here. The board members are elected every four years. The Board votes on all matters affecting the well-being of Tocabaga. Majority vote wins any debate and it cannot be voted on again for another year.

Most people living on Tocabaga carry a weapon. It's normal and totally expected to carry a gun because our second amendment rights permit us to do so. We do not tolerate traitors, spies, or Quislings. We all have a few things in common and that is the desire to remain free from Federal Government oppression and to protect our loved ones and friends.

I'm the oldest of three brothers. We grew up fighting bullies and gang members in a tough neighborhood in south Chicago. My Dad, one of the most honest men I have known, always stressed, tell the truth, and help each other. Never ever be a bully, never steal, and try to protect those who cannot protect themselves. I have always stood up for the people who could not defend themselves. I hate liars and bullies.

Standing 6 feet tall at 180 pounds, I am in great shape for my age and my body is honed by years of physical training. I keep in shape by lifting weights almost every day and running three miles four times a week. I shave my head two times a week as it is cooler in the hot south and wear a ball hat to keep the sun off my head. There's a two inch scar on my forehead from a knife fight years ago.

I spent four years in the Army as a Military Policeman, and became an expert in the use of handguns, rifles, shotguns, and hand-to-hand combat. My legs have skin grafts from burns due to an explosion when working for the DOD (Department of Defense) doing security work for seven years. I always carry my Glock 17 side arm and Black Bear Cold Steel fighting knife.

I love our country, freedom, my family, and friends. If anyone messes with my family, or my friends, justice will be swift and painful. I have no use for anyone who breaks the law, cheats, or steals. For the most part I follow the Ten Commandments, but also believe in The Code of Hammurabi which is an eye for an eye. I fight to keep our Bill of Rights under the United States Constitution.

That is me, Jack Gunn, a.k.a. Tocabaga Jack, and these are my chronicles.

I am Director of Security for Tocabaga Island. I live here along with 606 other Patriots. We're fighting to keep our freedom, our homes, and our families safe from the evil forces gone wild. Tocabaga is a sanctuary or safe haven. If you believe in the Constitution, the Bill of Rights, and are of good moral character you are welcome here.

We are waiting for you to contact us by email to find out where Tocabaga is located. Sending us an email is your first step to Freedom. There is an email address hidden in these chronicles. Tocabaga is a real location. I will reply.

RECAP OF JULY 5, 2025

Yesterday we killed BOKO KANG and a few of his men. During the mission one of our men, named Brogan, went MIA. We came back to find him because no one gets left behind. Arriving at the KANG camp we found they had pulled out hours ago. Tommy tracked them and found they were heading west on 22nd Avenue. The chase is on to find our missing man.

It hit me that the BOKO KANG gang might be coming to Tocabaga. It was the only place that they could obtain guns and food.

I informed my men, "Listen up, here's what I wanna do. I'll take one Hummer and follow the KANG gang down 22nd Avenue. Tommy and Jim Bo, you're with me. The rest of you head back to

Tocabaga and get ready for battle. If the DRAGON men come down the Road of Death let them have it. Anyone who wants to kill and eat us is going to die."

My men concurred and we headed back to the vehicles parked at the Armory. I decided to call Rico and warn him about the cannibals roaming around our area. Rico offered his help but I advised him to stay put and be on full alert. I informed him of my plan and the fact that they may be headed to Tocabaga.

My men headed back to the island while the three of us zoomed down 22nd Avenue after the gang. Along the way, every now and then, we saw a burning body or car. These bad guys would kill and burn anyone they saw.

We were going over the Pasadena Bridge to St. Petersburg Beach; which provides a clear view for about a half mile down the road. Tommy, standing in the gun turret, yelled, "Slow down! Stop! There's someone in the street about five hundred yards ahead."

I stopped and turned off the motor. Looking through his binoculars Tommy commented, "He has a yellow bandanna around his neck and an AK. He's a Dragon boy."

I coasted down the bridge with the motor

off, careful not to make any noise, and pulled off the road near some bushes behind an old rusted car. Out of sight we sat there for a few minutes visually searching the entire area for more people.

"Do you see anyone else?" I asked Tommy.

"Nope, no one else is around."

"What do you think he's doing by himself?"

"Maybe he's the rear guard. Let's capture him and find out what he knows."

I asked, "How we gonna to do that? If he's the rear guard then the main force must be close by."

"I'll shoot him with the 308. I'll just wound him. Using my silencer no one will hear the shots. Then we just drive up and question him, if he's still alive."

Jim Bo stated, "Sounds good, let's do it."

I nodded my head for Tommy to proceed.

Tommy dismounted and started creeping forward, keeping low using bushes for cover. He was within a hundred yards and laid prone on the ground to steady his aim.

Just as Tommy was taking aim the guy turned around and looked in our direction. Tommy had a perfect shot. POP ... the man was hit in the shoulder and dropped his AK47. He was knocked to the ground by the impact of the bullet. Then Tommy shot one of the guy's legs. He couldn't move and was ours for the taking.

The .308 caliber, 168 grain Bob Tailed Hollow Point cartridge, is a devastating round. At one hundred yards the velocity is 2,600 ft/sec. and it provides 2,670 lb/ ft of energy. It can kill an elephant with no problem.

I started the motor, picked up Tommy, and drove to the KANG boy. We jumped out with Jim Bo standing guard as Tommy and I stepped up to him. He was on the ground bleeding and writhing in pain. My guess was we didn't have long to question him, before he would bleed to death.

The DRAGON boy was about eighteen years old. He looked undernourished with sunken eyes and hollow cheeks. There was a two inch hole in his right shoulder and he was shot in one leg. The bullet hit his femoral artery and broke the femur bone. His leg was bent backwards in a grotesque manner and he was slowly bleeding out. He couldn't move his body, but twisted his head up to look at us. He mumbled in pain, "Why … y'all shoot me?"

I questioned him, "Where's your gang?"

"Mister, please help me." He was getting weaker by the second. Tommy tied a tourniquet around his leg. He yelled out in pain as the tourniquet was tightened to stop the bleeding.

"Ok, we stopped the bleeding. Now tell us where your gang is at?"

"They're at the hotel with the big tower. Man, give me some pain killer!"

I ordered, "Tell us where your DRAGON gang is going next."

"Man, I don't know. I'm just a soldier."

"Did you capture a man yesterday?"

"Yeah, we found a guy."

"Where's he at?"

"I don't know. Maybe he's dead. Who are you guys?"

"We're the guys who killed BOKO KANG last night," Tommy replied.

"You didn't kill the ... DRAGON. The DRAGON has many ... heads." The kid slumped over. The life had drained out of him so Tommy released the tourniquet and his blood flowed onto the sidewalk.

Tommy asked, "What the hell did he mean the DRAGON has many heads?"

"Damn, I don't know, but I do know you killed the DRAGON."

Tommy said, "Well, we know where they are, but we still don't know about Brogan. It's not looking good." Tom began to search his body. "Hey, this guy has a radio. I'll bring it along. Maybe we can use it."

The radio was a standard hand held model good for a six mile range at best. It was tuned to channel four.

Turning to Jim Bo, I said, "Grab his yellow bandanna and gun maybe we can use them." The sun was setting and the sky was turning bright orange. "It's getting late so let's go. We'll backtrack the way we came so no one spots us."

After washing the blood off our hands we mounted up and drove back to Tocabaga. Arriving at our sanctuary it was almost dark as we went to the bar for a drink. Tony was there and questioned me. "Did you find Brogan?"

"Sorry we didn't find him. We don't even know if he's alive. We captured one of the DRAGON boys and he told us that Brogan was probably dead. Right now the gang is at the old Tower Hotel."

"Well … let's go look for him. Every minute counts."

"It's late and we need some rest. We can't do any more today. The KANG group might come here tomorrow so we better be ready. Right now we can't do anything to help Brogan even if he's alive."

"Let's meet here at 9 a.m. and discuss what we'll do tomorrow."

We wound up the meeting and I went home to my wife and kids. I was too pooped to stay awake and fell into bed. The bed felt great, but as I lay there, thoughts of Brogan kept haunting me.

Tomorrow we might have a major battle with the DRAGON men, but I wasn't worried about that. We've defeated better gangs and even the Feds. What did that kid mean the DRAGON has many heads?

It really bugged me that Brogan was Missing in Action. Even if we find him how would we rescue him? Maybe we could make a trade of some kind. Maybe we'll need to use force to free our friend. I know one thing: I'll never give up looking for Brogan and neither will my men.

THOMAS H. WARD

JULY 6, 2025

After breakfast with the family my crew and I went to the gun safe located in my garage. We removed our M4 carbines, Glock hand-guns, and slipped on bullet proof vests. On top of that we wear our tactical vests. Everyone in my family wears the same identical combat gear and carries the same type of weapons. It's my policy that we all use the same weapons.

On the front left hand side of our tactical vests and on the back we wear a small Velcro American Flag. This allows us too quickly identify each other in the heat of combat and helps prevent being shot by friendly fire.

My crew is my family and close friends. We have practiced shooting and close-quarter combat techniques for years. We are a unit or team that can move and shoot together. We think alike because of years of training.

It was raining lightly and a big storm was headed our way. I could hear the thunder off in the distance and see the thunderheads rising in the sky. The four of us climbed into the Hummer and drove to the bar for the meeting.

Summer storms usually only last a few hours unless it's a big front or a tropical storm. Tropical storms can last for days and winds can reach up to 70 mph. We haven't had a hurricane here in 20 years, probably due to global climate change.

We have noticed the water level has only risen by a few inches but that's not a problem because we have at least two feet before it goes over the sea walls. Long term weather reports obtained from the Army inform us that global cooling is now taking place, not global warming. A new ice age is now forming. An ice age would mean that thousands of people would migrate to Florida to escape the freezing year-around weather.

Reports advise that the northern part of the United States could cool off very fast because the Gulf Stream has almost stopped flowing. The Gulf Stream carries the warm water to the northern east coast states, all the way to the Arctic Circle, and over to Europe. This is what keeps the Glaciers from growing out of control.

Back in 2010 when they were screaming that global warming was starting due to carbon dioxide levels increasing, they were completely wrong. It was the start of a natural cooling cycle that has been repeated since the beginning of time. Slight global warming always precedes the ice age.

We've noticed that it's not as hot here as it use to be. Normally in July temperatures would reach 98 degrees. Now it rarely goes over 94 degrees. So something is happening to the climate.

Looking at a map of the last ice age, which was about 13,000 years ago, the glaciers grew at an alarming rate and covered Canada down to the tip of Ohio. It is estimated that it only took a year for the temperature to drop to freezing. People can't live in those conditions for very long. Once the hoards of people start to migrate here it will cause major problems. Food and housing will be affected by the large increase in population.

I called the meeting to order. "Ok, I'm open to any suggestions as to what we should do to find Brogan." In attendance were Tony, Tommy, Ron, Jim Bo, Chris, and Rick. These are some of my best shooters and most trusted security team members.

Tommy advised, "If this storm gets worse then I suggest we make up a crew and go to the hotel and search for him when it gets dark."

"Why wait until dark?" Tony asked.

"Night is the best time to sneak and peek. The storm will help us move around without being noticed because most of their men will be inside or under cover."

"I say we go now. Let's have a vote." Tony raised his hand but no one else did.

Tommy said, "I've been on a hundred sniper missions. I'm not going in the day time, rain or no rain. I wanna stay alive and the best way to do that is at night." A few spoke up and stated that Tommy was right. Night is the best time to sneak around unseen.

"Alright we go tonight as soon as it gets dark," I advised. "Now let's make a detailed plan and decide who goes. My idea is to park two Hummers at the apex of the Beach Bridge. These will provide backup for us in case we need to make a fast exit. In addition I want two more men armed with M249 machine guns.

"Tommy you're in charge of the mission, so who do you want to tag along with you?"

"I only need you and Jim Bo."

Tony spoke up. "Hey, I'd like to come."

There was silence in the room. Tony is one of our best shooters, but he is not in the best of shape. Tony is a big guy at six feet four inches tall and pushes about 300 pounds. That makes him an easy target for the bad guys. When you're that big it's pretty hard to hide behind a small bush.

Tommy responded, "Tony, we need you to man a fifty on the bridge. We'll be moving fast and I don't want you to get captured. If they capture you they'll have a feast." Everyone laughed at that comment, but Tommy was serious.

"That's very funny, Tommy. However, I see your point so I'll man a fifty."

"Ok, good. The Hummers will drive us across the bridge and then we'll proceed on foot to the Tower Hotel. I suggest we take the beach and stay off the streets."

I replied, "I agree." Taking the beach will be tougher going because of the deep sand, but it will also be noiseless. It's about a five mile hike one way.

"We need to have suppressors on our M4s. Bring 200 rounds of ammunition, some water, and radios. We should tie a yellow bandanna around our necks to make us look like one of them. I'll bring the radio I found on the DRAGON boy. Are there any questions?" Tommy asked.

Looking at Tommy, Rick asked, "How long do you think the mission will take?"

"I guess about four hours, but who knows. You guys stay on the bridge no matter how long we're gone. We'll radio you to come and pick us up if we get in a bind."

"Roger that."

"Jim Bo and Dad, we'll wear our usual camouflage fatigues and black face paint. Ok, if nothing else we meet at the bridge at 8 p.m." We both nodded our heads. Our combat fatigues are breathable and wick the sweat off your body, while keeping you dry from the rain.

The meeting was adjourned and we went home to rest and have some lunch. There would be no dinner tonight. I never eat before going on a mission because I don't want any unexpected stops to relieve myself. Stopping to take a dump could get you killed.

I spent the time getting my gear ready and then played checkers with the grandkids. We sat on the patio watching and listening to the peaceful rain falling. There's something about the rain that makes you feel relaxed and cozy. It was agreed that Ron, my brother, would stay home and watch after the family.

The storm blew in and it was raining cats and dogs when 8 p.m. came around. Big rain drops were pouring down and the wind was gusting to 30 mph, almost blowing the rain sideways. The thunder was loud and continous, what we call rolling thunder. The rumble seems to never end. Every now and then we would hear a very loud crack and see the bright flash of a lightning strike. This weather would provide us a natural cover.

Standing in my garage, I checked Tommy for loose gear and then he checked us. We removed our American Flag patches and placed them in the gun safe. We were prepared for the wet weather with our water proof fatigues and combat boots. We each had M4s with sound suppressors' and of course our Glock side arms. I strapped on my Black Bear fighting knife which has saved my life more than once.

We smeared black camo paint on our faces and then slipped on our bullet proof vests putting the black tactical vests over top. Each of us tied a yellow bandanna around our necks identifying us as DRAGON men. We were traveling light with only 200 rounds of ammo and a gallon of water in our camel backs. All our gear and clothing probably weighed about Forty pounds.

We pulled up our collars and donned our boonie hats to keep the rain off our heads. Tony,

Chris, Rick, and Maggie walked up in the pouring rain. Maggie would operate one of the machine guns if needed. They were already soaked from the big pounding rain drops. The temperature had dropped to 60 degrees.

I commented, "You know, you're gonna freeze up on the bridge with the wind blowing. I'd wear some warmer clothes."

"We'll be ok if we stay in the Hummers," Rick commented.

I shook my head and said, "Mount up."

It was dark as we mounted up except for a lightning strike now and then. Our security guards wished us good luck as our trucks rumbled across the Tocabaga Bridge. Riding with Tony I told him, "Take us all the way across the Beach Bridge and then pull back to the apex and wait there. If you see anything give us a shout on channel fifteen."

"Roger that, if we see anything, we'll let you know."

"Stay awake and alert." Tony just nodded his head because he didn't like me telling him something so obvious.

The trucks stopped and the three of us dismounted. Maggie yelled, "Good luck guys." We jogged in a low crouch, towards the beach, passing by the old pink hotel. I recall that President Bush stayed there doing a visit years ago. It was a hotel for the rich and famous once, but now it's a home for the poor and Free Roamers. Most of the windows are broken and in this storm it must leak like a sieve.

CRACK … a bolt of lightning struck the water, a few hundred yards out in the gulf, and we all jumped from the noise, but kept heading north to the Tower.

The sand was wet and it stuck to our boots. Walking in wet sand is like walking with glue on your boots. It makes each step twice as difficult. Every step you take your foot slides backwards a little and impedes your forward progress.

Tommy had the point and Jim Bo the rear guard.

Jim Bo commented, "Walking in this shit is tough going."

I laughed and replied, "Wait until you gotta run in it." I used to run in the sand all the time to increase my endurance. I forgot how strenuous walking in the sand could be and found myself quickly out of breath. The rain was still beating down and visibility was only about 50 yards.

I heard thunder off in the distance but it sounded different. It sounded like a cannon or explosives. Tommy held up his hand signaling for us to halt. We stopped and gathered around him behind some bushes. He looked at me and said, "Did you hear that?"

"Yeah, it sounded like cannon fire," I replied.

"I didn't hear anything," Jim Bo commented.

"Listen." We heard it again. There were two distinct BOOMS.

We peered down the beach looking in both directions for flashes of light, but saw none. Tommy moved forward again with us following in his footsteps.

After 30 minutes we stopped and huddled together. Tommy advised us, "Check your guns, lock, and load."

Pulling out my camel-back hose, I took a big swig of water. The rain was not letting up, but at anytime it could. That's the way it rains here in Florida. It pours like crazy and then just stops.

Sitting on an old log that washed ashore, I looked up and saw a flash of light. Then I heard the … BOOM! I said, "Over there. I saw a flash of light right before the explosion."

"Where at?" Tommy inquired.

"Over there." I pointed at the water about a mile off shore.

"That's in the water. Are you sure?"

"I don't know. There's a lot of thunder and lightning. Maybe it was a reflection off the water. It's still raining hard so I'm not a hundred percent sure." Florida is the lightning capital of the United States. Each year a few people are killed by lightning in Florida.

The wind from the storm was blowing from the east-southeast which means the west side of the state, near the beach, would have smaller waves. Further out in the Gulf of Mexico the waves were probably 15 to 20 feet, but in shore they were running two to three feet.

"Let's push on," Tommy advised.

We had no sooner stood up and taken about 50 steps when Tommy whispered, "Get down, targets approaching."

We dropped down, lying flat, on the wet sand. Three men were running down the beach in our direction. As they came closer we could see they had guns and wore yellow bandannas. They kept stopping to look behind them, as if someone was chasing them.

Tommy pulled out his night vision

binoculars to have a look see. He softly said, "Four men are behind them. Maybe they're chasing them."

I commented, "Let's take them all out." Tommy concurred with a nod of the head and I tapped Jim Bo on the shoulder telling him to get ready.

Tommy advised, "I'll shoot all three of them. The last man gets it first." We agreed since Tom is our best shooter.

The DRAGON men were within 40 yards of our location. They would run right past us if we let them. Tommy took aim, and the last man fell, then the second in line. Finally after six steps the first man fell dead in the sand. They didn't even hear the shots.

Tommy whispered, "The next four men will be here in a couple of minutes. They're running four abreast. Jim Bo, you and Dad, shoot the two closest ones and I'll take the other two. When I fire you both fire." We agreed and waited for Tommy to take the first shot.

The four men approached out of the rainy darkness. We could tell they weren't DRAGON men by the beret caps and uniforms they wore. They looked like soldiers, but we didn't know whose soldiers. As their faces came into view from

20 yards away I could see they looked different but the rain distorted my vision.

Tommy opened fire and so did we. All four men dropped on the beach in three seconds. It was a perfect ambush. We jumped up and ran over to the bodies. Checking their pulses, we found one of the men still alive. He was stunned from rounds hitting his bullet proof vest. I picked up their guns and threw them in the water. I was shocked to see the Red Chinese Flag on their uniforms. I quickly scanned the beach to see if more men were coming.

Tommy grabbed the man still alive by his vest and pulled him up close looking directly in his face. He asked, "What the hell are you commies doing here?"

Tommy took out a zip tie and forced the guy's hands behind his back. He yelped in pain as Tommy bent his wounded left arm. I searched him for more weapons.

I checked his arm and the elbow was blown away making his it useless. I told Tom, "His arm is shot to shit."

Speaking in good, but broken English he told us, "The People's Republic of China here to claim Florida. It now belong China. Me, Captain Zhu Lei, of People's Expeditionary Marine Forces."

Judging by the tone of his voice he was

cocky bastard. I kept my gun pointed at his head. Just for the heck of it I hit him lightly in the head with the barrel of my carbine. I didn't like his tone and said, "You're full of shit. Red China doesn't own Florida."

In 1999 Red China took over the lease and control of the Panama Canal. They moved into Central America controlling the economy. In 2012 they became allies with Communist Cuba and started drilling for oil 70 miles off of Key West. Chinese gunboats became a common sight off the coast of Florida. There is only one reason China would want Florida and that's for the oil. Florida has a lot of oil reserves in the Gulf.

"US government owe China many trillion dollar … then default on payment. US now bankrupt. US President approve sale, Florida State to People's Republic of China. This cancel all debt. Debt paid in full. Florida now, Lotus Flower State. You must surrender. We your leaders. Surrender now I promise quick painless death." I laughed and hit him in the head a lot harder almost knocking him out.

Tommy warned me, "Don't knock him out. We need more information."

"How did you get here?" I asked him. He didn't reply so I hit him hard in his wounded arm.

He winced in pain and replied, "Boat."

"How many boats and what kind do you have?"

"I never tell, state secret." I believed him because he looked like one tough cookie who would endure any type of torture. He was a trained professional.

"Why were you chasing those men?" I bumped his head again with my gun barrel to refresh his memory.

"We saw fires. We land small crew. Want to find food. They not friendly. Attack us, killing five my men. My gun ship open fire, destroy them. Some run away. We chase them."

"Do you have any more men on shore?"

"Maybe yes, maybe no. My boat look for us."

Tommy told me, "Drag him over to the bushes. I'll run down the beach with Jim Bo and check it out."

As I forced him up and pushed him to the bushes he struggled and tried some Kung Fu kicks on me so I shoved my gun barrel into his mouth knocking out a few teeth in the process. After that he followed me like a little puppy dog to the high weeds and bushes. I had no sooner knocked him to the ground and a bright search light flashed from a boat offshore. They were scanning the beach looking for their men. I heard a radio crackle and a voice came on speaking in Chinese. "Zhu Lei, … #####". I don't know what they said, but I found a radio hidden in his shirt, turned it off, and put it in my pocket.

"See. They look for me. They not give up search."

"Do you expect the people of Florida will surrender to China?"

"Yes, US President approve it."

"You're mistaken. The President can't approve that." I thought even if the President did approve it, we the people wouldn't stand for it.

"What your name?"

I looked at him for a minute wondering if I should tell him. I observed his uniform was not in good shape and he looked skinny and not well fed. I think the People's Army is suffering from lack of supplies. His arm was bleeding and I could tell he was in a lot of pain.

"My name is Jack Gunn."

"You US Army, Mr. Jack?"

"I'm in the militia. We provide the law and order around here."

"You Policeman. Mr. Jack, you work for us. We give people equal rights. US people leave Florida, then ok. People stay, ok. They follow Chinese law. All ok."

The search light flashed by us and I could see the outline of the boat. It looked like a patrol boat and there was a cannon mounted on the bow. The rain was starting to let up.

I started to laugh at his statement and he asked, "What funny?"

"You don't know what you are up against. There are over five million people living in Florida and everyone has guns." I didn't tell him about the Special Forces, like the Rangers, operating in Florida. I didn't tell him about the gangs of cutthroats running around.

"We know about Florida. You know nothing about China."

"I know that every man and woman will fight to the death to stop China from taking over Florida."

Out of the blue he asked, "You been Disney World?"

"Man, you really don't know what's going

on in the United States. We're in a civil war. Disney World was destroyed a long time ago."

We sat there in silence for another half hour waiting for Tommy and Jim Bo to show up. Zhu seemed disappointed that there was no more Disney World. The patrol boat moved south still searching the beach for Zhu Lei.

Tommy ran up out of breath, dropped down to one knee, and said, "They're all dead or gone. We counted 123 bodies and saw five dead Chinese Marines. We checked each body to make sure Brogan wasn't there. The question is did the DRAGON men run north or south?"

I pulled out my radio, "Tony, keep a sharp eye, because the DRAGON boys maybe headed your way. We're on the way back now."

"Did you find Brogan?"

"Negative."

"I think the DRAGON boys are already here. There's a group of about 30 men near the pink hotel now. They're standing around in the parking lot. I think they spotted us."

"Yeah, maybe they're sizing you up. If they approach the bridge, start shooting. We'll be there in 45 minutes. Out for now."

Zhu asked, "Who DRAGON men?"

"Those are the men you had a fight with. They're cannibals. They kill and eat people." I didn't know if Zhu understood the word cannibals because he had a puzzled look on his face.

Jim Bo asked, "What are we going to do with this guy?"

Zhu was on his knees and Tommy was standing behind him. I saw Tommy point his gun at Zhu's head. "I got no use for these bastards. I fought them in Korea. They're sneaky little fuckers." With that comment he pulled the trigger. Zhu slumped over to the ground.

Tommy was in the last Korean War in 2016. This war purged North Korea of the communists and united Korea into one country again. The Chinese had some forces backing the North, but the North Korean Army didn't have the resources to fight a mass war and surrendered in 30 days.

I said, "I guess Zhu Lei won't get to see Disney World." No one laughed but me. I took his black beret with the Chinese Marine emblem on it and shoved it in my pocket. I wanted to show everyone what we were up against.

We jumped up and started to run back to the Hummers waiting on the bridge. None of us said a word about killing Zhu Lei. We all knew that sooner or later we would have to kill him. We could never bring him back to Tocabaga with us.

We jogged all the way back to the pink hotel and stopped while still on the beach. Peering around in the dark we carefully searched for other people. We didn't see anyone until we went around to the front of the hotel. The DRAGON men were standing in the parking lot. They were huddled together having some kind of meeting.

I ran across the street, in the shadows, and jumped into the mangrove trees on the side of the road. Jim Bo followed me and we covered Tommy as he came across. As he was crossing one man yelled, "Hey, there goes a guy!" All thirty of them turned and looked at the same time.

I yelled, "Jim Bo start shooting those assholes!" We opened fire and so did they. We were out gunned for sure, but Tommy made it to the trees without a scratch. Bullets were whizzing over head as we ducked and slowly moved out.

I got on the radio, "Tony bring both Hummers down here and open up on these jerks. We're trapped at the foot of the bridge, on the north side, in the mangrove trees."

"We're on the way!"

In a minute I heard the distinctive rapid … BAM, BAM, BAM … sound of the M2 machine guns. Rick's Hummer stopped right in front of us providing cover while we climbed inside. Rounds were harmlessly pinging off the skin of the bullet proof truck. Maggie, standing in the gun turret, was firing the fifty burning through rounds as fast as she could. I saw a few of the KANG boys drop to the ground.

Both vehicles' rapidly backed up to the apex and stopped firing. Tommy told everyone, "Get the M249s set up and when the gang is within 50 yards open fire." The five of us laid prone on the wet hard concrete surface waiting for them to attack. The rain and wind had subsided and all was quiet.

I had no doubt that the seven of us on the high ground, with four machine guns, could stop any attack they could muster. They were slowly coming for us, walking towards the foot of the bridge. They had no cover to hide behind. Were they that dumb or doped up to continue an attack after seeing our fire power?

The beach bridge is a four lane divided bridge with two lanes in each direction. One Hummer is sitting on each side. The DRAGONS split into two groups and were coming up each side of the bridge. Ten men approached, staying low, and they started to run up the bridge. The remaining men stayed behind them by a good distance.

They were within 50 yards and Tommy

yelled, "Open fire!"

Two fifty caliber machine guns and two M249 guns, all firing at the same time, make a hell of a noise. The evil boys were falling to the ground either because they were shot or to keep from being shot. They didn't stand a chance.

As the bodies fell Tommy, Jim Bo, and I would take aim with our M4s' and shoot them to make sure they were dead. Three minutes later I yelled, "Stop firing!"

Of the original ten not one man was left standing. The main group of about twenty men ran the other way and dispersed into the darkness. No one in our group was shot. I thanked God for his help.

Tommy wanted to go down and shoot each one in the head to make sure they were all dead. We drove down to the group of fallen bodies and stopped. Suddenly one man jumped up from behind a bridge pillar and frantically waved his arms in the air. He started yelling, "Don't shoot!"

He had no weapon but did have a yellow bandanna around his head. I shouted, "Hold your fire!" As he came towards me his shape looked familiar in the dark. He came closer and we took aim. When he was fifty feet away I ordered, "Stop right there! Get on your knees. Keep your hands in the air."

"Jack, for crying out loud, don't shoot! It's me … Brogan!"

"Brogan, you dumb ass!" I ran towards him as did the whole crew, except for Maggie who kept an eye on the walking dead just in case one woke up. Tony picked up Brogan and gave him a big bear hug as we all slapped him on the back.

"Man you're one lucky SOB," Tommy said, as he gave him a man hug. "Stand over there with Tony while we finish making sure these jerks are dead."

Tommy walked around shooting each man in the head. Then he advised, "Let's leave the bodies here as a warning. If any other DRAGONS or the Red Chinese happen by they'll think twice before coming over the bridge."

"Good idea," I replied. "Let's get Brogan home and checked out by Doc Scott. Rick, I'd like you and Maggie to stay here on guard until day break. Then I'll send someone to relieve you."

"No problem, whatever you say Jack," Maggie stated, which didn't allow Rick any choice in the matter. He was stuck on guard duty for another seven hours like it or not.

We all squeezed into the one vehicle and

headed home. It's a short fifteen minute ride to the bar and the clinic which is right next door. Brogan said, "I need a double shot of JD and a smoke." We dismounted and headed into the bar while Chris went to find Doc Scott.

The only bar on Tocabaga has been here since 1993. It's old and smells like mildew and smoke. The inside hasn't been painted in over 20 years so the walls are a dirty brown color. It's a small bar about 1,000 square feet in size. The actual bar is "U" shaped and covered in tile. The floor is also tile and easy to keep clean. The metal bar chairs are in need of repair. The bar is air-conditioned thanks to the solar generators that the Army provided. We have refrigeration to keep food and drinks cold. We brew our own beer and wine. The other day a couple of old timers made some moon shine. We obtained our whiskey from the Army Rangers. Where they got it from we don't know. One day they just showed up with a truck load of booze.

When off duty everyone hangs out at the bar. It's the place where news and gossip gets passed on. There are many debates or discussions on the direction of the country. Tony is the guy that keeps the bar running. He also locks it up at night to keep the real drunks from hurting themselves by over indulgence.

I looked closely at Brogan. I couldn't believe it was him. He lost some weight and was a dirty mess, but other than that he appeared in one piece. He had grown a short beard, so he didn't even look like Brogan. I noticed that he wore dirty jeans and a blood stained blue shirt with the yellow bandana on his head.

I took the bandana off his head and told him, "You won't need this anymore DRAGON boy. Doc will check out that cut on our head. It looks infected."

Brogan touched it and winced a little. "Yeah, it's infected alright."

Tommy poured a double shot of JD for everyone and handed the first one to Brogan. After jugging down the golden liquid in one gulp, Brogan pounded the glass on the bar stating, "Give me another one." Tommy filled it up again.

Raising his shot glass, Tommy toasted, "Welcome home Dragon boy." Everyone cracked up and repeated, welcome home. "We thought you were a goner. Tell us what happen."

"It takes a lot to kill me. It's a good thing you guys came along when you did because I was just getting ready to kill the whole gang by myself." Everyone chuckled.

Tommy poured us all another drink while

waiting for Brogan to tell his story. "I was looking under the water for my glasses when I heard Tommy and Jack run across the water. Then I heard shots. I found my glasses and hid in the water until the KANG boys ran past me. One guy came walking up the river bank, very close to me, so I shot him. I took his gun and clothes. Look at the bullet hole." He stuck his finger through the blood stained hole in the blue shirt and wiggled it.

"Lucky for me he was my size. Knowing I was surrounded, and couldn't escape, I figured I'd blend in with them. I pushed his body downstream and hid my guns. I put his yellow bandanna on my head and walked into their camp like I was one of them."

"Shit, you just walked into their camp? That took balls. Then what happened?" Tony asked.

Brogan was thinking as I handed him a smoke and lit it for him. Taking a deep drag he exhaled a white smoke ring. Coughing a little Brogan took a sip of whiskey. "Man, nothing tastes as good as a smoke with a shot of booze.

"I walked right up to the club house and saw the men that you killed. Everyone was running around and didn't know what to do. One guy asked me who I was. I told him, Brogan and asked him his name. He told me he was Jackson. He didn't say another word to me and walked away." That comment cracked us up. Only Brogan could do that and get away with it.

"I thought I found your broken glasses near the club house," I stated.

"Those weren't my glasses. These are mine. Anyway after your sniper attack the gang decided to move to another location. I tried to slip away from them, but they had guards watching everyone. They always had a few men watching everyone to prevent desertions."

"Brogan, did we kill the DRAGON?" Tommy asked.

"Yes and no. There are two more men who look alike and wear the yellow turban which means they're the leaders. These men look like twin brothers. They look like the guy you killed. Maybe they were triplets."

"That's what the kid meant when he told us the DRAGON had many heads."

"Yeah, I guess he does have many heads. Anyhow, we went to the old Tower Hotel and made camp there. It started to rain and the storm blew in. Most of the men were standing under cover on the outdoor patio. I tried to stay away from everyone and moved around to a place out of the rain and wind. I didn't want anyone asking me a lot of questions.

"Oh, I had another guy ask me my name. I told him I was a friend of Jackson. He didn't bother me anymore after that. I guess Jackson was some kind of boss."

"Brogan, what if they would have went north instead of south?" I asked.

"I didn't think of that at the time. Anyway, I was sitting there planning to escape somehow during the storm. I kept edging further and further from the main group. That's when the shit hit the fan."

Brogan slammed his glass down again on the bar and Tony poured him another shot. I gave him one of my smokes which he gladly accepted.

"What happen next?" Chris asked.

"Hold your horses while I light this smoke. Where was I? Oh yeah, I was just getting ready to make a run for it and a guard saw me in the bushes and asked me what I was doing. I told him, taking a piss. Then BOOM, BOOM, a boat started firing a cannon at us and strafing the whole area with machine guns. Half the gang was killed in a few minutes and the rest were running for the hills. I hid behind a wall and watched ten soldiers come ashore in boats. They started shooting everyone."

Just then Doc Scott walked in and wanted a drink. Doc stood on the side listening to the story.

Brogan looked at Doc and continued, "I decided to make a run for it. I jumped up and took off heading for Tocabaga. I wasn't alone however; some of the men were following me, running down the street like scarred rabbits. I was like their leader.

"Hey, Tony, you got anything to eat? I'll like a beer also."

"Keep talking. I'll get you something," Tony replied.

"Ok, where was I?" Brogan was getting a little drunk from the four double shots.

"You were running down the street trying to get away," Tom advised.

"Oh, yeah. I'm running down the street trying to get away and a young guy runs up next to me and asks, 'where are we going?' I started to laugh because I knew where I was going but he didn't. I told him, 'I'm getting the hell out of here.' I tried to outrun them but the gang stayed right on my heels until I ran out of breath at the hotel. We all stopped and fell to the ground exhausted."

Tony handed Brogan a beer and gave him a couple pieces of cold fried chicken with some beans. Brogan gobbled it down in a minute and almost choked in the process. After taking a big swig of beer he let out a loud belch. We sat there waiting for him to finish the story.

"As we sat in the parking lot the same guy comes over to me and asks, 'now what boss?' I'm sitting there trying to think how to shake these guys when I see your Hummer sitting on top of the bridge. Then a short time later I see Jack run across the street. I thought you guys had found me and were going to pull off some kind of rescue."

"We thought you were dead," Tommy commented.

"Well, I'm not dead. Then I saw Jim Bo run across the street and I tried to distract the gang from looking that way, but one jerk saw Tommy run across and the shooting started. I thought I was a goner because I know what great shots y'all are. I ducked and laid on the ground waiting for the bullets to stop flying."

"What made the gang attack us on the bridge after they saw the Hummers with all our fire power?" Tony inquired, while handing us all another round of drinks.

One of the men said, 'Let's get those bastards.' Most of them were doped up on meth or PCP and just do whatever they're told to do. The next thing I knew they were walking to the bridge. I knew you would kill them all so I made sure I was in the back of the group. I tried to hide behind someone for cover. When you guys started shooting I fell to the ground and crawled behind a pillar. I pulled a dead guy on top of me for added protection."

"Man, you're lucky. We almost killed you," Jim Bo stated.

"Yeah, I'm lucky, but I told you I can't be killed." That was the most foolish statement I heard him say. Maybe it was the booze talking.

"Do you know where the rest of the KANG men went?" I asked.

"No, I don't. I don't know who the soldiers were in the boat that killed everyone."

"Oh, you'll be happy to know they're Chinese Marines. They came to rescue you." The room broke up into uncontrolled laughter.

"Hey, what's so funny?"

While laughing I replied, "Oh nothing, but up until now we only had DRAGON boys to contend with and now we got the Red Chinese to combat. The Chinese are here claiming that Florida belongs to them. We may have to fight the whole fricking Chinese Army."

"How's that possible," Brogan slurred, barely keeping awake from all the drinks.

"We captured a Chinese Marine Captain and he told us that the President gave Florida to China to pay off the US debt." Everyone was still laughing. The idea was so insane it was funny.

I pulled the black beret out of my pocket, threw it on the bar, and said, "Here. Look at this." Everyone stopped laughing and slowly examined the hat.

Doc Scott who hardly ever becomes involved in a conversion, said, "That's total bull shit. The President doesn't have the power to do that! That's HIGH TREASON and punishable by death. In Chinese it's called PAN GUO ZUI, a crime of high treason." Doc had studied the Chinese language while in college years ago. It might come in handy if we capture any more Chinese soldiers.

"Doc, we all know that. The problem is; what are we going to do about it? I gotta call Captain Sessions and let him know what's going on. Maybe he already knows what the President did, but I don't think he knows we have Red Chinese right here in your backyard. I'll see you guys tomorrow. I have to make that call and get some rest."

Doc said, "I'll stick around and fix Brogan's head while he's out."

I looked at Brogan and he was passed out. His head was laying on the bar in puddle of his own saliva. I laughed as I walked out and drove the Hummer home with Tommy and Jim Bo. I was happy Brogan was home and alive.

On the way to the house I called Sessions. Sessions didn't have any good news. He knew about the Chinese agreement to take over Florida. He didn't know they were already here. He advised me that Drones would scout the Gulf waters and the east coast of Florida looking for any Chinese boats. Then he would provide us an update as to what we're facing. In the meantime he told us to stop any Chinese Marines at all costs and don't let them gain a foothold in our area. Sessions told me he'd have a report by tomorrow.

Arriving at home I took a shower and put on some clean clothes. The wives made us some food and we told them we found Brogan. We advised them that the Red Chinese were here and it may mean everyone will have to fight to save Tocabaga. Our wives were speechless and wanted to know why the Army wasn't here to help us. I didn't have any good answers for them and went to bed.

I thought if the Chinese have any air support or a large number of troops we're in deep shit. We didn't stand much chance against a well armed force of 3,000 or more trained Marines especially if they have gunboats, planes, or choppers.

The DRAGON men are no longer a threat to us in my opinion. The Red Chinese are the major threat. We need to obtain better weapons and increase the size of our forces. Tomorrow we'll start training everyone on Tocabaga how to use a rifle. I'll call Rico and coordinate with him to booster our defense forces.

My guess is they'll try to land here to gain a foothold and then move east to Tampa to take control of SOCOM HQ. That would give them control of the only large useable airport in our area.

The President of the United States has lost his mind. He has shown his true communist colors. He's dangerous and clearly wants to destroy the country. He has committed HIGH TREASON. The Military has to step in now, in full force, to remove him from office since our Congress is doing nothing to stop him.

JULY 7, 2025

My radio woke me up. It was Rick screaming, "Jack, come in!"

I picked it up, "What's up?" I rubbed my eyes and looked outside. The sun was just coming up.

"Jack, we got trouble. There are two Red Chinese gunboats in Pass-a-Grille Channel."

"How big are they and what are they doing?"

"They're just sitting there. I guess about a 100 feet long. Each one has a cannon and it looks like two big machine guns on the rear deck."

"Ok, I'll check it out. Don't do anything until you hear from me."

"Roger that."

Just then my security radio came on again. "Jack, Mike here. I confirm there are two gunboats sitting in the middle of the channel. I'm on the west side of the island looking at them right now."

"Mike, what are they doing?"

Mike or as we call him Army Mike, is a retired Command Sergeant. He's a big muscular guy who works out all the time. Everyone likes him and trusts his judgment. Mike fought in every major military conflict over the last 15 years and knows how to use every weapon system.

"It looks like they're forming a landing party. There's about twenty men on each boat making ready to come ashore."

"Do you think an MK153 could take out those boats?"

"Hell yeah! Good idea."

"Ok, I'll bring them over ASAP. If any men disembark shoot them when they're within range."

"Ok, hurry up."

"Roger that Mike, just hold down the Fort."

All of the security people heard the radio call and I knew that everyone was moving to their assigned locations on the island. We have a total of

120 soldiers including the Amazon Warriors.

I jumped out of bed and started yelling for Tommy, Jim Bo, and Ron to get ready for combat. I grabbed a cup of java after putting on my gear and started for the door when my wife Hemmi yelled, "Jack, be careful it's a jungle out there. Come back alive or don't come back."

I laughed and replied, "Don't worry Honey." This was a standing joke she made with me every time I went into battle. I don't recall where she picked this up, but I always thought it was funny because it didn't make any sense. The odd thing is she never laughed about it like I did. Maybe she's serious.

We jumped into the Hummer and drove to our only bank which is now our armory. Three MK153 SMAWs were stored there in the big old vault. At last count we had thirty reloads. This is the most powerful weapon in our ordnance.

The MK153 SMAW means Shoulder-launched, Muti-purpose Assault Weapon. This is a hand held shoulder fired missile system used to blow up vehicles, boats, and buildings. A very powerful weapon that is reusable. You fire a missile and put in a new one.

As we loaded the three missile systems and ten rockets into the Hummer, people came running up asking what was going on. I told them go to your assigned location or go home and stay there until we give the all-clear.

While driving to the westside guard post I phoned Captain Sessions and advised him of the situation. Sessions told me, "The Drones spotted four more gunboats in the Gulf south of you near Ft. Myers. They're 134 foot Shanghai Class gunboats with a 37 mm rapid fire cannon and four heavy machine guns. Each boat carries 20 Marines along with a crew of 23. They're old boats and don't have modern armor plating."

In 2007 the Shanghai Class gunboats were transferred to the China Coast Guard and refitted as Ocean Patrol Boats. The superstructure was heavily modified. Armament was reduced to one rapid fire cannon forward and 4 heavy machine guns. Some of the freed space was used to stow small patrol boats and add extra quarters.

I asked Sessions, "Do you think we can take them out with an MK153?"

"Yes, it can take out the boats but it may take a couple of rounds to do it. Remember the effective range is about 500 yards. I'll send armed Drones to eliminate the boats near Ft. Myers."

"Ok, please do that. We'll take care of the two here. The Chinese are getting ready to come ashore. They have no idea that we're waiting for them."

"Roger that, Jack. Good luck and keep me advised."

Pass-a-Grille Channel is a shallow channel that's more or less a small harbor. The water is calm and it's a safe port during a storm. That's probably why the boats came into this channel, but they may have also missed the main channel which goes into Tampa Bay. That might have been their real destination.

The radio crackled and it was Rick, "What's going on, Jack?"

"We're on the way to the westside guard post now. Sessions advised me to use our MK153 rockets to blow up the boats. Once we fire I want Maggie to use that fifty and terminate anyone in the water that comes your way. Don't let them come ashore."

Maggie replied, "Don't worry, Jack. We'll get those little bastards."

From the top of the beach bridge the fifty

could reach out and hit anyone heading north trying to escape. Our hidden allies were the sharks that rove these waters. We unintentionally trained them to expect fresh meat by dumping the bodies of our enemies into the local waters.

We pulled up to the guard post and Army Mike helped us unload the rockets. It was around 6 a.m. and the sun was just coming up. There were fifteen men along the seawall hidden by the thick green shrubs. We had three M249 machine guns at the ready. Mike commented, "Hurry up. They're getting ready to come ashore."

I instructed the men, "Mike, you take one of the MK153s' and Tommy take one. Jim Bo, you and Ron, do the reloading. Fire at least two missiles into each boat at midships, above the water line. Machine gunners fire at anyone still alive in the water. Open fire on my command."

I crawled up to the seawall to have my first look at these gunboats. Peering out from the foliage I could see they were at least 100 feet long. The Red Chinese commie flag was flying on each boat. It was important to hit them first before they could fire their cannons or machine guns. I observed soldiers were starting to load into small boats.

I shouted, "Rick and Tommy make ready to fire. Take careful aim, make it count. Ready … FIRE!" Mike fired first and a split second later

Tommy fired at his target. The rockets roared away creating a stream of smoke giving away our position.

The missiles streaked toward their targets about 400 yards away. KABOOM ... KABOOM ... both rockets hit the targets right at midships, just above the water line. They blew big gaping holes in the side of both ships. The MK153s' were reloaded and they fired again.

Watching through my binoculars both rockets hit home. The second missile Tommy fired went in the same hole and the ship blew up into two pieces. It must have hit the magazine compartment, because the humongous explosion lifted the boat out of the water. The shock wave from the massive explosion blew my hat off.

I saw the other gunboat swing its cannon in our direction. I yelled, "Everyone duck. Incoming fire!" Then BOOM ... BOOM ... BOOM, in rapid fire, the 37 mm rounds hit the house right behind us. The explosions knocked most of us to the ground. We scampered several hundred feet away as the boat was still firing.

It must have fired twenty rounds before Mike yelled, "Reload me!" I saw Ron grab a rocket and reload the MK153. Mike knelt on the seawall while taking aim and fired. It was a perfect hit. The gun turret exploded in a ball of fire. We shouted for joy!

Many of the commies were in the water, but there was one little boat with about ten men speeding away, heading north, trying to get out of our range. They were headed for certain death. Maggie opened up with the big fifty caliber M2 machine gun from on top of the bridge. They didn't stand a chance of escaping. I watched the little rubber boat sink while Maggie kept shooting until all the men disappeared from the surface of the water. Soon shark fins broke the surface of the water. They were attracted by the smell of blood.

The gunboats were slowly sinking in the middle of the channel. They were done for, but there were still 20 men trying to swim to safety. They were smart and managed to hide behind the sinking boats blocking our line of fire. I got on the radio to Maggie. "Can you reach those guys?"

"No, they're out of range."

"Ok, watch where they go. We'll have to hunt them down. I'll be there shortly.

"Tommy, Mike, there's about 20 men going ashore on Pass-a-Grille. Let's take two SAWs and go find them." They each picked up a SAW and followed me. "Steve and Bill, I need you both on this mission. Follow us over to Pass-a-Grille."

We were mounting up and Mike said, "Wait, let's take along an MK153 just in case." He ran over and picked up a launcher with three rockets. After safely loading them in the Hummer we took off. I thought that was a good idea because you never know when you might need big fire power.

We arrived on top the bridge pulling up next to Rick and Maggie. I asked them, "How many men came ashore, and where did they go?"

Rick replied, "There were about 20 men. They went ashore near that big palm tree." Rick pointed to a tree a good 800 yards away.

Maggie corrected Rick, "There were exactly 18 men, not twenty. The exact count is important. Right, Jack?"

"That's right, Maggie." Rick gave her a disgusted look. I could imagine after being with Maggie for seven or more hours that Rick was ready to go home.

Including me, we have a total of eight fighters. I didn't like the odds, but we know the area and have some big guns. I figured that evened up the odds a little. There is only one road in and out of Pass-a-Grille. The problem is there are a lot of old buildings and places to hide. The last thing I wanted to do was go searching house to house because that's a sure way to get killed.

"Anyone got any ideas how we should hunt these guys down," I asked the group.

"We should snipe them," Tommy answered.

"I agree," Army Mike concurred. "We let them come to us. They can't go south because it's a peninsula. They can't swim anywhere. They have to come north sooner or later."

I replied, "Yeah, and chances are they'll run into some Free Roamers in the area and have a gun fight with them." We all started to laugh because the Free Roamers were ruthless killers. They were most likely hidden all over Pass-a-Grille.

We could still hear rifle fire coming from Tocabaga. It seems some commies were still alive, trying to swim away from our shooters.

I continued, "Ok, let's think this thing out. I don't want anyone getting killed today. We know there's only one road out. Since they're on foot they could move down the beach or the channel side. If I were them I'd go down the beach since it is further away. In any case we need to cover all three zones, the street, beach, and channel side."

Mike suggested, "Let's set up two man sniper teams. Two men to cover the beach and two men watch the channel. That leaves four men to cover the street along with the two Hummers. The Hummers can move in for the kill if the sniper teams spot them."

"Alright that sounds like a good plan. I suggest we set up the teams about 50 yards south of the pink hotel. That's the narrowest part of the peninsula. We can put two men watching the street, two on the beach, and one with each Hummer. We'll keep the trucks hidden out of view. Everyone agree?" All the warriors nodded yes in approval.

Tommy spoke up, "Jim Bo and I will cover the beach."

"Ok, I'll take Bill and cover the channel side," Mike responded.

I commented, "That leaves Maggie, Steve, Rick, and I to cover the street. Maggie and I will take the street. Steve, you and Rick, each take a truck. Hide them off the road and sit tight. If there aren't any questions let's move out."

No one had a question so we mounted up in the Hummers and drove to our location. The sniper teams spread out to find good cover. Each team had one M249 light machine gun. Steve and Rick did a bang up job hiding the trucks behind some high bushes. Maggie and I took positions covering the street.

We hunkered down between some Azalea bushes which provided a good view of the street. We were well hidden. Sitting next to me, Maggie asked, "Which way do you think they'll go?"

"If I was them I'd take the beach. They have no place to go but north. Maybe they have a radio and can contact a boat but I think they're too far away for a hand held radio. It might be possible to contact a boat if they can get to a high spot, like the top of the hotel."

We heard faint automatic weapon fire coming from downtown Pass-a-Grille. I could tell they were AK47s. Then we heard an explosion which sounded like a hand grenade. It was clear that the Chinese Marines had run into some Free Roamers. Free Roamers might be cutthroat killers, but they're still Americans. They don't like being told what to do and certainly won't take kindly to seeing Red Chinese troops here.

I got on the radio, "If anyone spots someone let me know."

The radio hissed. "Should we shoot Free Roamers?" Tommy asked.

"Yes, of course. They're all dangerous."

Maggie said, "Fire ants are biting me. They're all over this area."

These tiny little ants bite the shit out of you. The bites itch and turn into a red welt, like a typical bug bite. Then after several hours the red welt gets a tiny white head in the center. If you scratch it they become infected.

"Yeah, let's move." We got up to relocate and brushed the ants off of each other. Maggie and I were going to feel some pain from all the ant bites. I wanted to take off my clothes and rinse off the bites.

Sitting down again I asked, "Maggie, you ok now?"

"Yeah, but a shower would be great. Maybe we can take a dip in the Gulf later."

"A nice skinny dip sounds good to me."

Maggie smiled while looking at me and said, "Yep, that's exactly what I had in mind."

"How's it working out with Lisa?"

Lisa was Rico's girlfriend who just came to live on Tocabaga the other day. She's staying with Maggie while she learns the ropes.

"Lisa is doing great. She really knows how to knife fight. She's pretty good with a gun also. There's only one problem."

"Oh, what's that?"

"She is a sex maniac. All she ever talks about is sex and you. Jack, do you have some kind of relationship with her? I wouldn't blame you if you do, because she's pretty hot looking. I think she's in love with you."

"She looks at me like a father figure."

"Oh, I don't' think so. You should hear her talk about you."

"What does she say?"

"She says stuff like, I love Jack. I wish he'd come over alone, so I could prove it to him. Are you sure you're not involved with her."

"I like her alright, but she's just a good friend. She'll get over me and find someone on Tocabaga. Maybe Sergeant Willis would date her."

Maggie looked at me to see if I was telling the truth. She's known me a long time so she could tell if I was lying. I lit up a smoke and sat back trying to take the edge off.

"Lisa told me she danced totally nude for you. Do you expect me to believe you didn't do anything with her dancing around naked?"

"What are you? My wife? Lisa didn't tell you the whole story of what really happened."

"Oh! She told me alright. She told me a lot."

I took another puff off my smoke and looked at Maggie's face. She looked angry and frustrated. Off in the distance I heard more shots. They seemed to be getting closer.

"Maggie, if I didn't know better … I'd think you were jealous."

Maggie started to laugh and then suddenly stopped. "You're right, Jack. I am jealous. I never told you this before but after Robbie was killed you were the only one that helped me out. You made me feel better by giving me the farm to run and making me a Captain of the Amazons. You gave me hope and something to live for. Now I'm helping the whole island. I owe you big time."

Maggie reached over, grabbed me by the shirt, and pulled us together. She kissed my cheek and gave me a tight hug. Maggie is a woman in her late thirties and used to be the best looking woman on Tocabaga until Lisa came along. She has long dark brown hair and a perfect body which she keeps in tip top shape. I give her a ten, but it's not her looks that matter so much. It's the way she acts and moves. She's just plain sexy and tough as nails.

"Maggie you don't owe me anything. You've worked hard and risked your life. There are only three women I trust to cover my back, my wife, my daughter, and you."

"What about Lisa? You don't trust her to cover your back?"

"No, not yet. I don't know her well enough.

Hey, that's enough woman talk. Let's concentrate on our job." Suddenly, we heard shots a few blocks away. "Stay alert Maggie, they're getting closer."

I looked at my watch and it was now almost two in the afternoon. Chances were the Red Chinese are waiting for dark to move down the beach off of Pass-a-Grille. We sat there on full alert. Every noise we heard Maggie raised her weapon and looked thought the rifle scope.

I clicked the radio and asked, "Everyone still there?"

"Beach team, ok."

"Channel team, ok."

"Hummer one and two, ok."

Maggie asked, "You got any food, Jack? I haven't had anything to eat all day."

"Yep, I have some energy bars." I tossed her a couple and opened one up for myself. "Bon appétit."

The energy bars were given to us by the Army Rangers. One bar is like eating a full meal. It keeps you powered up for about four hours. The only problem is they don't taste so great.

It was a typical hot summer day and the humidity was higher than normal due to the rain last night. Maggie and I were both drenched in sweat. I took my boonie hat off, filled it with water, and dumped it over Maggie's head to cool her off. We both laughed as she returned the favor. I knew that when night came, we would get ate up by mosquitoes. They were already biting my hands and face.

"You got any bug spray, Maggie?"

"Nope, but I wish I did. I'm getting bit up."

Mosquitoes are the worst bugs. The little blood suckers carry all kinds of diseases like, West Nile Virus, Meningitis, Malaria, Yellow Fever, Dengue Fever, Encephalitis, and Chikungunya. Chikungunya is a new one that came from Africa. It causes a fever and excruciating joint pain for several weeks which totally knocks you on your ass.

"Maggie, let's cover our faces with mud and that will help prevent bites."

"Good idea, I need a facial anyway." We made some mud and covered each others' face. When the mud dried it would provide some good protection.

It was getting dark. I stood up, walked over to a bush, and took a leak. Maggie said, "Now you did it."

"Did what?"

"You took a leak. Now, I have to take one."

"Well, go ahead, don't let me stop you. I won't peek."

As Maggie got up and walked past me she replied, "Ha Ha, Jack."

"Hey, don't wander off too far. The bogie men are out there." It was almost dark and all you could see were shadows. Maggie moved off through the bush and out of view.

It was calm and you could hear a pin drop. She was gone about five minutes when I heard a twig snap over in her direction and then another. Someone definitely stepped on a twig. Someone was moving in the jungle and it wasn't Maggie.

I stood up and started to move towards her direction, but stopped when I heard a rustling sound from bushes about 60 feet away. I didn't dare call her name because it might not be her. It could be Free Roamers or the Reds.

I knelt down, raised my M4, and looked through my FLIR night scope. I saw two men sneaking up behind Maggie. Just as she stood up and reached down to pull up her pants they jumped her. One man put his arms around her from behind and covered her mouth. The other picked up her gun and hit her in the face. I saw her slump, she was out cold.

I couldn't fire because of all the dense

foliage. My bullets could be deflected and I might hit Maggie by accident. I moved around them to obtain an open shot.

I could hear them softly speaking. They were Free Roamers. One man said, "Look what we got."

"Yeah, she's a cutie. I haven't had a piece of ass in months. Let's do her."

The other guy said, "Do her right here? No, let's tie her up and take her back to camp. We can all have some fun."

"No, I wanna do her right now!" I watched him pull Maggie's pants down to her ankles. I saw the jerk lay his gun down and unbuckle his pants. The other dirtbag stood there watching holding on to his AK. I had to act fast.

I slowly moved closer being very careful not to make any noise. I spotted a rock about the size of a baseball, as they came into view, so I picked it up. I threw the rock over their heads to make them turn around and look in the opposite direction. Thud … it hit the ground; they quickly turned around to see what made the noise.

I jumped out from behind the bush and fired my silenced M4 hitting the man holding the gun twice in the back. He dropped dead as a door nail to the jungle floor. The other dirtbag darted for his rifle, but tripped falling to his knees while trying to pull up his pants.

Sitting on the ground he looked at me, and then at his gun, trying to decide if he had time to grab his AK47 before I shot him. I said, "Go ahead dork, make my day."

He didn't listen to me and I kept walking closer to him. "I told you to go for your gun."

He held his hands up in the air. "Mister, please don't kill me. I didn't mean any harm."

Without saying another word I pulled the trigger ... POP! I placed one shot right between his eyes and he slumped over dead.

"I didn't mean any harm," I told his dead body. I must admit it made me feel good killing two disgusting dorks that were going to rape Maggie.

Bending down I splashed some water on Maggie's face and shook her. She had an ugly welt on her left cheek, but other than that she appeared fine. "Maggie wake up."

As I held her head in my lap she slowly opened her eyes and asked, "What happened?"

"Free Roamers jumped you."

Maggie sat there stunned for a few moments. She noticed her pants were pulled down to her ankles. She looked around and saw the two dead dorks. Maggie asked, "Did they do anything?"

Holding her head up I gave her a drink of water and said, "Do you think I'd let any shit heads touch you." Using my wet bandanna I gently wiped off her face. "You'll have a sore jaw for a while, but you'll be ok.

I held up two fingers and asked, "How many fingers?"

"Two."

"Is your vision blurry?"

"No, I can see fine." Maggie touched her jaw and felt the large welt on her cheek. She winced a little from the pain. Regaining her senses she stood up, pulled up her pants, and brushed off the dirt. "Thanks for saving my life."

"You don't need to thank me."

"When they first jumped me, I thought it was you fooling around."

"Maggie, you know I don't fool around."

"I know, but sometimes, just sometimes, I wish you would, Mr. Perfect."

"Come on, let's cover up these bodies and get back to our position." We covered up the bodies with big fallen palm fronds. I was concerned that some wild dogs or coyotes would smell the blood and come over for a free dinner. I didn't want any rabid dogs roaming around near us.

Sitting at our post we heard gunfire over by the beach. It sounded like AKs' on full auto. My radio hissed, "We got someone firing on the beach. It looks like the Chinese and the Roamers are fighting. They're headed this way," Tommy advised.

Clicking the radio button I asked, "Can you see anyone?"

"Negative, not yet. I think they're skirting the fringe of the beach using the bushes for cover."

"Yeah, that makes sense. How far away are they?"

"I guess 200 yards and closing."

"We need an ambush plan. You got any ideas." Tommy didn't reply right away.

We knew there were 18 Chinese, but we didn't know how many Free Roamers they were fighting. I thought it was great they were killing each other, making our job easier.

I added, "Tommy, what if we back off and just watch these guys kill each other?"

"Yeah, we could do that but we run the risk of some of them escaping. I was hoping we could find an officer alive and grill him for information.

Put him on the hot seat so to speak."

"I see your point. So what do you wanna do? We're running out of time."

"Ok, everyone listen up. We'll do an "L" shaped ambush. Jim Bo and I will be behind a big sand dune here. We're the small part of the L. Put one Hummer at one end of your leg and another one at the other end. Space them about 100 yards apart to create a machine gun cross fire.

"The rest of you space out 20 yards apart in between the Hummers. Stay undercover about 30 yards from the beach. Our beach fire should drive them towards you. When you spot them, open fire. Anyone got any questions?" No one answered.

I directed the Hummers into position. Mike and Bill came over and we made a defensive line in between the two gun trucks at 20 yards apart.

We looked for trees or logs to hide behind. Maggie was on my right and Mike was on my left. I had visual contact with Maggie and could see she was well protected behind a big old palm tree.

I hunkered down, on the ground, behind a dead tree. I had just laid down when I heard the distinct sound of a rattlesnake. There's no mistaking the sound of a rattlesnake. I've heard them many times. I tried not to make any sudden moves. The snake sounded very close to my left side. I slowly turned to look and there it was three feet away. It was coiled ready to strike. Judging by the size of the rattle, sticking up in the air, it was a big snake.

If I made any sudden movements it would strike. I couldn't swing my M4 around for fear the movement would set off the snake. I couldn't use my hand gun because it didn't have any noise suppression. The shot could give us away.

I slowly took off my boonie hat and tossed it right on top of the snake's head as it struck. It struck the hat two times. I jumped up and shot it six times with my M4 making sure it was dead. I hate snakes and that scared the shit out of me. Picking it up by the tail I threw it into the weeds, hoping there weren't any more crawling around. I tossed my hat into the weeds because there maybe venom on the fabric and you don't want that in your eyes.

I heard radio static and Tommy came on. "They're getting closer. As soon as they're all in the ambush zone we'll open fire. Using my night vision I can see your Hummers. You guys all set up?"

I replied, "Roger that. How many men do you see?"

"I see ten Chinese and six Free Roamers. That means eight Chinese might have been killed or they're still out there."

"The Roamers did a good job for us."

We could see the flashes from the gun barrels right in front of us. Looking through my scope I counted five men, then eight, then ten, and following close behind them, taking pot shots, were the Roamers. Everyone was now in our ambush zone.

I clicked the radio, "Everyone is in our zone. Open fire." I squeezed the trigger and so did everyone else. The plan went kind of backwards, but it still worked out. Since my group fired first that forced the enemy to run out onto the open beach making thcm easy targets for Tommy and Jim Bo.

I heard our beach guns open up. Looking through my FLIR I saw the Roamers start to run back the way they came. I saw a few of them fall as our machine guns spit out fire and death from their barrels. The foliage and bushes in front of us were blasted away by the wall of bullets giving us a more-or-less an open view of the beach.

Tommy yelled on the radio, "Cease fire! Cease fire! They're flying a white flag and want to surrender. Pull the Hummers out on the beach to cover these guys."

I heard Tommy yell, "Drop your guns, and put your hands in the air! Get on your knees!" The Hummers pulled out of the jungle onto the beach keeping the Red Chinese covered. The rest of us followed and surrounded the Reds. The man holding the white flag looked like some kind of officer.

I told Tony, "Keep an eye out for the Roamers." Tony swung the machine gun turret around to cover our backs.

To my surprise only two of the Red Chinese had been wounded. Tommy and Jim Bo walked up to each person and checked them for weapons. They found several hand grenades, rifles, a couple of pistols, and knives. We threw everything into the Gulf of Mexico. Jim Bo tied their hands behind their backs using plastic flex handcuffs.

The leader had on one of those old fashion military hats. He was dressed in a fancy uniform; like one you would wear in a parade. Tommy asked him, "What's your name?"

"My name is General Chen of the People's Republic of China." He spoke in a defiant manner and judging by his gray hair he appeared to be about fifty years old. His oversized belly told me he ate too much and was not in the best of shape. I guessed he was tired of running so he surrendered.

Tommy looked at the guy next to Chen. "What's your name?"

"Captain Kim, head of security for the

General. I demand you treat us with all due respect as specified under the Geneva Convention."

Kim had on combat fatigues and so did the rest of his men. Their uniforms looked almost new. He had a hardened face, almost weather beaten in appearance. He was lean and seemed to be in great shape. His men looked identical to him. I could tell these guys were real warriors and had been in some battles. Judging by their faces they weren't happy about being captured.

The Geneva Conventions comprise four treaties that establish the international laws for the humanitarian treatment of prisoners, be they military or civilians. The treaties were ratified by 196 countries.

I responded, "You're not in a position to demand anything Captain Crunch. We don't follow the Geneva Convention here. Kim is a Korean name. What are you doing in the Chinese Military?"

"After the second Korean War many of us moved to China and enlisted in the Chinese Army. It is the only type of work we know."

Tommy stepped over to me and signaled Mike and Jim Bo over. He whispered, "These men are an elite guard for the General. We have an important guy here. We need to take the General and Captain back to the Fort and interrogate them."

I asked, "What about the other men?"

"I don't want any of them around. We only have the two Hummers for transportation, so we can' take them all. Leave them here tied up on the beach for the Roamers to get. I'll take one Hummer, with Jack and Maggie, along with the two officers. We'll leave first and when we're out of sight, you guys bug out."

Our Hummers can only carry five people at one time. With the prisoners we have five men in our truck. That leaves five of our people to load into the other one. Steve's pickup is parked on the bridge which could hold all the prisoners but we didn't want ten dangerous men on Tocabaga. Tommy was right; leave them here for the Free Roamers to kill.

Riding back to Tocabaga, the Captain asked, "What about my men."

"Don't worry. We'll take good care of them," Tommy advised.

The General asked, "Are you in the US Army?"

While driving I answered, "No. We're local militia."

Maggie was turned around in the front seat pointing her M4 at the General and he commented,

"You know, your President made an agreement with China. He gave the State of Florida to my government to pay off the US debt."

"We know all about that. One of your men, Zhu, told us. What the President did isn't legal," I told him.

"You know Captain Zhu Lei? He's one of our best."

"The best at what? Chinese checkers?" We all laughed, but Kim and Chen didn't think it was so funny.

"Where is Captain Lei now?"

"Captain Lei went to Never-Never Land at Disney World."

"What do you mean? He would never leave his men and disobey orders."

"I mean Zhu Lei is dead."

"Dead? Who killed him?"

Tommy said, "I killed him. You'll be happy to know he didn't suffer. Now shut up, Chen! Maggie, blindfold them so they can't see anything."

She covered their eyes with bandannas before we crossed the bridge onto Tocabaga. Tommy stopped at the bar to let Maggie out. He told her, "Find Lisa and Trini. Tell them to report for guard duty at the Fort ASAP."

I told Maggie, "After you find them go get some rest. You've been on duty for more than 24 hours."

"Thanks, I need a shower and some sleep."

We drove to the Fort and took them to the cement lined jail cell. This cell was the original jail built in 1898. It has a big two inch thick iron door with a small viewing port, but the only view you have is that of a concrete wall. There's one commode, a sink, shower, and four beds located along the wall. The room has no air conditioning. It's impossible to escape from this sweat-box dungeon.

Tommy pushed them both into the cell, removed the blindfolds, and cut off the plastic flex handcuffs, while I kept my M4 pointed at them. I locked the door as Chen stated, "This is not acceptable accommodations for officers. It's dirty and there are insects here."

"Too bad, it's all we have. I'll get you a broom to clean it out," I responded.

Chen kept ranting, "I will report you for mistreatment of officers!"

Captain Crunch asked, "Where are my men being held?"

We walked away while they yelled, and went to the air-conditioned radio room. We sat down for a much needed rest in the ice cold room. Tommy pulled out two bottles of cold water from the small refrigerator and tossed me one.

I took a big swig and said, "I'll take our new friends some water just to be nice." I picked up four plastic bottles and walked back to their cell. I wanted to squeeze some more information out of them

I looked inside the cell and they were resting on the beds. "Hey, you want some water?"

They sat up and looked at me. Chen said, "Yes please, and some food if you don't mind." I opened the little sliding door used for the transfer of food and dropped in four bottles with a couple of power bars.

"That's all I can give you for now."

Chen came up to the window and asked, "What is your name, sir?"

"Jack Gunn."

"Well Mr. Jack … if you take special care of us, I'll see that you are rewarded for your trouble. It's just a matter of time before my troops rescue me."

The Chinese always mix up the last and first

names because in their language the last name comes first.

"How are your troops going to find you?"

"Oh, they know where I am at all the time." Right then, I knew they had GPS locators hidden somewhere in their bodies. We'll have to strip these guys down and scan them for the GPS bugs. Doc Scott will have to cut them out.

"Where are my men being held," Captain Kim asked.

"Don't worry Captain Chopsticks, they're safe."

"You are a very arrogant person, Mr. Jack. You Americans think you're so great. You should cooperate with us because China will take over Florida."

"That's not working out so well. Like I told Zhu Lei, your best Chinese checker player, there are over five million people living in Florida and most of us have guns. We'll never let China take over our state."

I walked away and didn't say another word to them. At the radio room I advised Tommy about the possible hidden GPS units. I told him, "Go find a metal scanner and Doc Scott. We need to cut the things out of their bodies tonight. Oh, and bring back Jim Bo and Mike for extra security.

Tommy was just leaving when Trini arrived with Lisa. "Jack, you wanted us for guard duty," Lisa said.

"Yeah that's right."

"What are we guarding?" Trini asked.

"Two Chinese soldiers. One is a general, and the other a captain. They're over in the brig right now."

Trini laughed and giggled a little. "Do you want us to … like let them escape … and then kill them?" Lisa laughed along with Trini.

Trini had already killed one prisoner, in cold blood, trying to escape or so she claimed. I couldn't prove it one way or the other and really didn't give a shit, but these guys we needed to keep alive.

"No ladies, I need them alive. I want you to stand guard outside the cell. Don't talk to them, don't even look at them. You both got that?"

"Yes, Sir," they replied.

"One more thing. No one, and I mean no one, is allowed to see the prisoners without my permission. If anyone comes around contact me right away. I need to talk to Captain Sessions, so I'll be here if you need me."

They left the room and I knew that my Amazon Warriors wouldn't let anyone near our important prisoners. They take their job very seriously.

I got on the phone with Captain Sessions. It was a few minutes after midnight.

JULY 8, 2025

AFTER MIDNIGHT

"Captain, its Jack. Sorry to brother you, but I have a situation here."

"What's the problem?"

"We captured two Chinese officers. One is a general and the other a captain. He's really a North Korean who's in the Chinese Army."

"What's the generals name?"

"Chen, General Chen."

"Ok, I'll check him out and let you know what I find.

"Did your men sink the gun boats?" Sessions asked.

"Yeah, the MK153 rockets worked well. Chen and some of his men managed to abandon ship before it sank and swam ashore. That's how we captured them."

"Good work, so everything is under control."

I thought for a minute before responding. "Yes and no. There still might be some Chinese troops over on Pass-a-Grille. We'll check that out tomorrow."

"Roger that. I'll arrange for a chopper to pick up the prisoners and take them to SOCOM for interrogation. It may take a while before I can free one up."

"What about the Chinese Navy? Are there any more ships around Florida?"

"Our drones sank three of four gunboats. One managed to shoot down our two combat Drones, so you still have one boat on West Coast. We're sending two more Drones after that boat in the morning. The Chinese now occupy Key West and may start to move north on Route 1. We estimate there are currently 1,000 troops with four tanks."

"Oh, by the way I think the general has a GPS bug in his body. We're going to remove it."

"He probably does. Check under his right arm, near the arm pit. That's where they usually put them."

"Will do, Captain. Let me know when the chopper is on the way."

I had just hung up when Lisa walked in. "What do you need, Lisa?"

"I told Trini, I needed to take a leak. I wanted talk to you alone."

"Talk about what?"

"You don't pay any attention to me. You don't stop by to see how I'm doing."

"Well, I'm a little busy and haven't had time."

Lisa moved close to me and sat on top of the desk. In the dim light I could see her fatigues were skin tight. She had the first three shirt buttons undone revealing she was braless. She leaned over and gave me a peck on the cheek. I got up from the desk and stepped several feet away.

"Lisa, get back to guard duty."

"I will, but I just want you to know I need a man and you're the man I want."

"We already talked about this. I'm married and nothing is going to change that."

"I'm not asking you to change that. I don't wanna marry you. I'll just wanna be your friend with benefits."

I looked at her and took a deep breath. "Give it up, Lisa. Gossip around here travels fast and if my wife found out that we had a relationship she would kill me. Now get back to guard duty before I write you up for leaving your post."

The office door opened and in came Tommy along with Doc Scott, Jim Bo, and Mike. They all stopped and looked at Lisa sitting on the desk so I blurted out, "Ok, Lisa, if nothing else, get back to guard duty."

"Alright, see you later." Everyone eyeballed her as she swayed out of the room.

Mike watched her butt wiggle out the door and said, "Man, this is turning into a long day." We all laughed and agreed.

I said, "Mike, you're not married, so why don't' you take Lisa out and have a drink."

"I thought she was your girl. That's the rumor going around because you brought her to Tocabaga."

"Shit! Who started that rumor? Lisa is just a friend and nothing else. Pass that around to everyone."

"If that's the case, maybe I will ask her out for a drink."

Doc Scott said, "Heck, I might ask her out for a drink."

Doc Scott is a good guy, but he's a big nerd. He has jet black hair, stands about five foot four, and wears big black-rimmed glasses. He never goes out in the sun so his skin is almost pasty white. He kinda looks like a vampire. Doc doesn't have a girlfriend because there's not too much to pick from on Tocabaga. I don't think Doc is Lisa's type.

"Go ahead and ask her, Doc. What do you got to lose?" I told him. Everyone in the room snickered because they knew Doc didn't stand a chance of hooking up with Lisa.

"I just got off the phone with Sessions and he said to check under the right arm pit for a GPS bug."

Tommy asked, "Who do you want to check first?"

"Let's check Kim first. We'll separate them and take him to an officer's room."

"What if he doesn't cooperate?" Doc asked.

Tommy replied, "Then we make him. Let's get this over with so I can get some sleep."

Lisa and Trini where standing in front of the

jail as we went to the door. I peeked in the window and it seemed that the General was asleep, but Captain Kim was awake. I waved him over to the door. "Captain, we want you to come with us."

"What are you going to do, stick bamboo slivers under my fingernails?"

"We don't torture people here. We just kill them," Tommy advised him.

"I give you my word. I will fully cooperate and answer any questions."

I unlocked the rusty old door and swung it open. Tommy stepped forward with some flex cuffs and Kim said almost in a whisper, "There's no need for those. I will fully cooperate. Let's go now and not wake the General."

This tough guy is folding like a paper tiger and I wondered why? What did he have up his sleeve? Tommy kept his M4 pointed at Kim the whole time.

Jim Bo opened the door to one of the trailer living quarters. It smelled like mildew. He turned on the AC as Kim walked in and sat down on the bed. The five of us just looked at him because we were all surprised by his cooperation.

Kim looked at me and said in Korean, "Put' agŭl tŭrŏ chushigessŭmnikka? (Will you do me a favor?)"

I hesitated for a moment, wondering how he knew I could understand Korean, and said, "Amado, kŭrŏk'e hageasŭmnida. (Maybe, I will.)" I immediately wondered what the he was going to ask. "Speak in English Captain, so everyone can understand."

"First of all my name is not Kim. My real name is Colonel Park, Kang-Dae of the South Korean Army. I'm a South Korean, spying on the Chinese Army, for the Korean Intelligence Agency (KIA). Please hear me out. I know you Jack Gunn. Your Master, Yoon, Im Un, is my Master. Master Yoon told me many stories about Jack Gunn in Korea. You are somewhat famous among the martial arts schools."

I was shocked by Kim's comments. He knew my Master and he knew I spoke Korean. He must be telling the truth. I spent years in Korea while working for the DOD. I studied the ancient art of Hapkido, which is a form of judo combined with karate, under Master Yoon. I also trained in Tang Soo Do, a more violent form of Tae Kwon Do. I fought in many exhibition matches around the country.

"Ok, Captain or Colonel, tell me one story so I'll know if you're telling the truth."

"You once had an exhibition fight in Itaewon. You fought three men, all at one time and won the fight in the second round by TKO. Master Yoon told me it was a truly impressive fight. He told me you're the best student he ever had and you're an honorable man."

Itaewon neighborhood is located next to the US Army base in Seoul. Because of the base this part of the city is a big party location. It's full of bars, strip clubs, social clubs, and other places where you can get into trouble. It's a big tourist trap with cheap shopping. You can find whatever you want in Itaewon.

I replied, "Yes, that's a true story. How is Master Yoon these days?"

"I haven't seen Master Yoon since the war. I'm pretty sure his school is still in business. I remember seeing your picture on the wall of fame."

"Colonel Park, how can I verify your story?"

"All records of me and my men have been expunged. We've been undercover in China for five years. There is only one man who can verify what I've told you. He's in charge of the KIA and his name is General Park. He's my Father."

While living in Korea I became infatuated

with the country that the Japanese called the garlic eaters. In Korea garlic is served with every meal. Most of the food contains garlic and they eat whole cloves grilled or raw. South Korea is the only country that practices Confucianism and Buddhism.

Confucianism is lifestyle for one to live by. This lifestyle is actually taught in schools and at home. Confucianism was started in China by Philosopher Confucius also known was Kong Qiu. Under Mao, who started Communism, everyone was ordered to stop teaching it as well as Buddhism. Buddhism is a religion based on the life and teachings of Buddha.

Another unique aspect about Korea is the language. Speaking Korean is more like speaking German than Chinese. It has many multi-syllable long words. Korean writing has an actual alphabet like English does. However, Korean alphabet letters don't look like English letters. They appear to be more like Chinese, but are squared block-shaped letters. Japanese and Chinese don't have an alphabet but use symbols or characters for writing. People think these languages are all the same, but Korean is entirely different from any language on earth.

The Korean people are friendly and very trustworthy. For the most part they are non-violent because of Confucianism teachings and Buddhism.

However, if threaten, they will defend themselves.

I recall that during the Vietnam War only one other country fought on the ground with the United States and that was the South Korean Army. They were feared by the enemy because they were so ruthless. The South Korean soldiers are some of the best in the world. They should be because our special forces trained them.

"I'll send your picture and prints to SOCOM. Maybe someone from there will contact General Park at the KIA to confirm your story. Colonel, I'm honored that you know so much about me. We however, know nothing about you."

"Yes, of course, but I'll tell you everything," Park said.

"Ok, that's great. After we talk, we'll interrogate General Chen to confirm your story."

"That will not be possible because he's dead. I killed him when he was sleeping. Don't worry, I know everything about the invasion plan. Chen trusted me fully. I know every detail about his plan."

"Why did you kill him?" I was very concerned and sat on the edge of my seat waiting for his reply.

Park started to ring his hands together. I noticed his right eye was twitching as he replied, "There was no need to keep him alive. We have a saying; the only good commie is a dead commie. He would have lied to you anyway. You can trust me to tell the truth."

"Do you or General Chen have GPS bugs in your bodies?"

"You mean these?" Park pulled out of his pocket two tiny metal devices and gave them to me. "I cut them out after I killed him." Colonel Park took off his shirt and raised his arm showing a small bloody hole. Park was lean but very muscular. His upper body had a lot of scars from years of fighting. Judging by his body odor he needed a shower.

"How did you cut those out?"

"I used a plastic bottle cap. I scraped it on the cement floor, making a little blade."

"Doc, put something on Park's cut so it doesn't get infected." Doc reached in his bag of tricks, pulled out some type of cream, and applied it to the seeping hold. Then he covered the wound with a band aid.

Holding the bugs in my hand I looked at them. They were larger than other devices I had seen. "What's the range of these bugs?" I asked.

Park advised, "They can be picked up from twenty miles away if the weather is right. Put them in a metal box or wrap aluminum foil around them and that blocks the signal."

I asked Mike to send Lisa and Trini to get us some food, and beer. We were all hungry and needed to recharge. The sun was just peeking through the window shade. I had to decide what to do with Colonel Park.

"Let's move to the mess hall and wait for the chow," I told everyone.

We sat down in the empty mess hall and Park commented, "This is a typical Army mess hall. Do you have any troops here?"

I replied, "Yes, we do, Mr. Park. Army Rangers are based here."

"My Father is called Mr. Park. Just call me KD. It's short for Kang-Dae. Where are all the Rangers?"

"Sorry, that's confidential information. KD, tell us how you became a spy."

"To make a long story short, I just put on a North Korean Captain's uniform, walked across the border and asked to join the Chinese Army with my men. We told them we were once security for the Great Leader of North Korea. Of course we all speak fluent Chinese and English. We spent years training for this mission."

Park took a deep breath and continued. "After a few years in the Chinese Army we were assigned as security for General Chen. He was not very well liked by his men so he preferred to use Koreans for his security. He was worried about getting killed by his own men while sleeping." We laughed a little about that.

"Let me get this straight. The men on the beach with you, are also spies?"

"Yes, those are all my men. Where are they at now? I would like to see them."

"KD, I don't know how to tell you this, but we left them on the beach tied up. We thought you were all commies. We left them for the Roamers to kill."

"Who are these Roamers?"

"The Roamers are small groups of men who kill and steal from the helpless. They have no special training and aren't military. They were the men chasing you down the beach."

"I wouldn't worry about my men. They can take care of themselves, even with their hands tied behind them. Can we find them after we eat?"

"Sure we'll find them. Tommy, arrange to

have two Hummers with four men in each one. We'll need a pick-up truck to bring back his men."

"Ok, I'll be back in a flash. Just save some food for me," Tommy told us.

I asked Park. "Why didn't you tell me who you were sooner?"

"I didn't know who you were and besides, who would believe me. When you told us your name, I searched my memory. I knew I heard your name before. Then it hit me who you were while I was sitting in the cell. It's amazing that I ended up here."

"Yeah, it's a small world alright."

Trini and Lisa came in the room and placed plates of hard boiled eggs, smoked fish, oranges, and six beers on the table. Lisa looked at Park sitting there and asked, "Isn't this guy a Chinese prisoner?"

I laughed and said, "It's a long story, but I think he's a friend. Before you report for duty on Tocabaga take a picture of General Chen and get his fingerprints for me. Then dump his body into shark channel. You're dismissed."

Trini asked, "You mean the other guy is dead."

"Yeah he's dead."

The Warriors left the room without saying another word, but I could tell by their facial expressions they were disappointed and wanted to stick around. They wanted to find out what was going on.

It's a Korean custom to give your guest a drink first. I opened 2 cans of beer, and while handing him one, said, "Geonbae." We clinked cans together and he repeated Geonbae which means cheers.

"Maekju mas-inneŭn! (The beer is delicious.)," Park commented.

"Ok, tell us what the Chinese are planning. Help yourself to the food."

He grabbed a greasy chicken leg. Stuffing his mouth full of food, KD began to speak. "Excuse me, but I haven't eaten in a few days. On the ship we ran out of food supplies the day before you sank us. We pulled into this harbor to find food."

As he spoke pieces of food flew from his mouth. "One problem the Chinese Military has is a shortage of food. Their logistics is terrible." Koreans aren't much on proper western eating etiquette.

"Yeah, I can imagine their logistics aren't the best," I replied.

"Jack, you already know the Chinese want Florida for the oil reserves. They plan to drill on-shore and off-shore for oil. They don't care about the environment and will turn Florida into one big dirty oil well."

Doc commented, "That would create a real disaster. It would affect the drinking water."

In Florida the drinking water comes from underground springs or rivers. If they're contaminated with chemicals and oil then everyone will suffer.

Park continued, "The two boats you sunk were the tip of the spear. General Chen was in charge of the whole operation called Lotus Flower State. The Chinese plan was to explore the coasts and map out good landing locations. We were dropping off teams of men who would provide intelligence on the local areas. Their jobs were to locate any hot spots or areas that have a high degree of local militia that could cause resistance."

Park stopped talking, peeled an orange ever so gently, and took a bite. "Florida oranges are really good." He wiped his hands off on his shirt after eating. "If you look at the map of Florida you can see what they want to do. The northern border is Interstate 10 which runs across north Florida. They will secure the northern border and all major highways. Troops will land in the north at

Jacksonville and Tallahassee. Then they'll move south on the Interstate Routes. Troops have already landed in Key West and will move up Route 1 and Interstate 95 and 75 after securing the Keys.

"Most of your population is in the coastal areas and Central Florida. Troops will be landed in Tampa and Daytona. They'll move across the state using Interstate 4 and converge in the middle of the state around Orlando. Once the invasion is completed then all the Green Zones will be handed over to the Red Army. Any people living there will be under Chinese control."

"What's the time table for this invasion?" I inquired.

"Well, technically it has already started since troops are in Key West now. The other troop landings may take place in about two months. General Chen hadn't set an exact date because he was awaiting the arrival of the main force from China. No one knows when that will be. They'll stop in Cuba first for a little R&R before coming to Florida. It's a long boat ride from China.

"Our group was doing exploration of the west coast. We were testing and probing the area for any hostile actions. Your President promised the Chinese that U.S. people would gladly surrender if the Chinese promised a fair and just government.

We all know that the Red Chinese aren't going to be fair and just.

"They didn't count on such a high level of resistance. The General was shocked that you sunk two gunboats with no problem. He didn't even have time to send a complete message. He only stated we were under attack. Any questions?"

"So far it makes a lot of sense. How many troops do they plan to use for the invasion?" I asked.

"There are 1,000 in Key West now. They'll land another 5,000 in Miami. In the north they'll land 5,000 near Tallahassee and Jacksonville to close the border. Landing in Tampa there'll be about 3,000 and the same for Daytona Beach. I guess about twenty two thousand total troops."

"Are you sure about that?"

"Yeah, but they'll also have some armored vehicles for ground support operations."

I took a swig of beer and asked, "What about naval and air support?"

"They have or had ten gunboats and five landing ships. Other than that there is no naval support. As far as air support they have twenty chopper gunships based in Cuba. They're old and are always breaking down. I don't think they'll present too much of a problem. You can easily shoot them down with your missiles or RPGs."

"What's their biggest weakness?"

"Oh, that's easy. Like I told you, they don't have enough food. The Army will be put ashore with two days of supplies. After that they have to forage and loot for food. They have to live off the land so to speak. You can be sure the Army will kill and loot to obtain any necessary supplies."

"Now that General Chen is dead who will replace him?"

"That's a good question. Probably his second in command General Lim who is based in Cuba. Personally I don't think Lim can handle the job."

"Why not?"

"Lim is not the sharpest pencil in the box. China has a lot of problems and he won't receive the necessary support. They have food shortages all over the country. A silent revolution is taking place. Shortages of heating oil and gasoline are upsetting the people.

"There are Islamic extremists in western China along the Kazakhstan border. They have problems along the Russian border. Red China is at war with India over the Tibetan Plateau for control of the water. Then they need to keep troops in Cuba to prevent any revolution there. Red China can't spare anymore troops or resources to invade Florida."

"That's good for us. They're stretched to the limit."

Tommy walked in and advised us the trucks where ready. I was recording everything that Park told us on my cell phone. I needed to send this information to Captain Sessions. We finished eating and mounted up to search for Colonel Park's men. It was almost 10 o'clock.

Leaving the Fort, we passed by the camp ground and farming area. KD asked, "Do you grow your own food here?"

"Yes, we do. We're pretty much self sufficient," I informed him.

We crossed over the bridge at shark channel which had two guards on duty. Moving on to Tocabaga Island we came to the downtown area. KD said, "Wow, you have a nice set up here. Is this an island?" I stopped the truck to let Park look around and let off Doc Scott.

"Yeah, Tocabaga and the Fort are both islands," Mike told him. "We have guards posted 24-7 around the whole thing. It's impossible for anyone to breach our security." Park nodded his head with a smirk on his face.

"How many guards do you have?" Park inquired.

Tommy butted in and replied, "We have enough to protect everyone." I could tell that Tommy didn't necessarily trust Park. I also had some reservations and didn't want to tell him too much information until I had his story verified by SOCOM.

I emailed Captain Sessions all the information that Park had told us. We moved out over the Tocabaga Bridge. Nine men were posted on guard duty. I am sure Park made a point to count them. Reaching the old dilapidated condos Park stated, "I can tell you've had some big battles here."

"Yeah we've had a few," I advised. Park looked at everything. He took in every detail because he was a trained spy.

We approached the top of the beach bridge and stopped to survey the situation before proceeding. Yesterday we left 10 dead bodies on the bridge and now all that remained was some torn clothing along with a few half eaten body parts.

I was driving the lead Hummer with Park riding shotgun. In the back was Army Mike with Tommy in the gun turret. We dismounted and had a meeting to discuss our next steps. I put the

American Flag on the antenna so we wouldn't be mistaken for Red Chinese. Even the Free Roamers know better than to mess with us.

We drove to the beach where we left his men. I would radio the others when we found the Koreans or if we ran into trouble. I really didn't expect to find Park's men alive.

When we reached the beach Colonel Park started yelling out his window, "Annyŏunghaseyo (Hello)." I drove slowly down the beach and stopped at the location where we left his men. Park and I jumped out and found the plastic flex cuffs laying in the sand. I counted eight of them which meant all his men had somehow removed the cuffs. Doing some quick math in my head, I recalled that originally there were eighteen men that came ashore. We captured ten which included Park and Chen. That left eight from the captured group and eight from the original group for a total of sixteen missing men.

I commented to Park, "Originally we saw eighteen men come ashore with you. There were ten of you at the beach. What happened to the other eight men? Do you know where they went?"

Park advised, "We split into two groups. I'm sure they're all around here somewhere, but they could be dead. Maybe those Roamers did get them."

Park started yelling in Korean again. After a few minutes he stopped and said, "Maybe they followed us to the Army base."

"How could they do that?" I asked.

"Believe me they could."

"You're telling me they could be at the Fort right now or on Tocabaga."

"Yes, that's right and it could be very dangerous for your people." I wanted to say something, but I knew these Korean Special Forces were some of the best trained warriors in the world. Park was right; my men could be in real danger.

I said, "Well if that's true then let's drive back over the bridge and slowly go down the road looking for them. Park, yell out along the way, because they could be hiding anywhere."

I told Jim Bo to stay on the bridge with his crew to keep an eye out for Park's men. We proceeded back over the bridge with the pickup truck following.

Park said, "Let me out. I'll walk on foot so they can see me." I stopped and let him out. He yelled, "Lieutenant Lee! Annyŏunghaseyo!" We followed in the Hummer about 30 feet behind him. I started yelling out the window towards the other side of the road.

Passing by the old destroyed buildings we reached the intersection of Bayway South which is the only road leading to Tocabaga. Park walked over to me shaking his head and stated, "No luck so far."

"Maybe they're in a building around here waiting for night. We can't check them all. That would take days and it's dangerous," I told him.

Park said, "If you don't mind, let's sit here a while. Let me think a little." Park sat down on a block of concrete that was at one time the cement corner of a building. We all dismounted and I pulled out a smoke to take a break. I then walked to the other side of the road closer to Tom.

Tommy came over and said, "Man, it's a hot one today." There wasn't a cloud in the bright blue sky. He took a drink of warm water.

I asked Tommy, "Well, what do you think?"

"I don't trust Park at all."

"Why not?"

"I don't know exactly, but there's something about him that makes me feel uneasy. I can't put my finger on it."

"I agree with Tommy," Mike commented. "It seems a little weird that this guy knows who you are."

"I agree with you both," I stated. I pulled out my phone and called Captain Sessions to make sure he received my previous message. I told him the whole story and sent Park's picture to him. Sessions advised me he would pass this on to SOCOM and check out Park's story. I stressed we needed to know ASAP if Park is really working for the Korean Intelligence Agency.

Park started walking over to us and Tommy whispered, "If his men are as good as he says they won't move around until it's dark."

Park walked up and said, "My men must be hidden and won't come out until it's dark. I'd like to walk back to the island to obtain a first-hand view of the terrain."

"Ok, let's go," I replied. I radioed Jim Bo to withdraw from the beach bridge and return to Tocabaga.

Park and I walked down the concrete road full of potholes from cannon fire as the sun beat down. I was carrying all my gear and sweating my ass off. Park looked at me and said, "If you like I can carry something." He reached for my M4.

He had hold of it before I could stop him. I warned him, "Mr. Park, let go of my weapon."

"No it's ok, I'm happy to help you. If you don't trust me unload it."

"Park, let go now!" I would never unload my weapon and hand it to him. He let go and I could feel the tension in the air. "Park, I can't let you handle any weapons until I receive confirmation of your story from SOCOM."

"I understand you don't trust me yet. You know if I wanted to I could take that gun from you at anytime."

I stepped back a few paces not believing he challenged me. I looked directly into his dark brown eyes and told him, "KD, your ego is too big." The little prick just threatened me and I didn't like it one bit.

"You're correct. I guess … I've been with the Red Chinese too long. It has changed my thinking. I apologize for my rude comment. I should be grateful that you didn't kill us on the beach."

"Apology accepted. Whose idea was it to surrender?" I asked.

"General Chen wanted to surrender. He couldn't run any more. My men would have never surrendered."

"Did you ever fight Master Chen?"

"No, I never fought him." Now I really wondered about Park because every person is required to fight the Master before graduation.

I told Park. "My birth sign is a Dog and so was Master Chen's." All the students knew Master Chen was a Monkey. Master Chen made it a point to know the birth signs of all his students.

"My sign is a Rat." A Rat was probably a good match. Park is a sneaky rat. He didn't correct me about Chen's birth sign. He either forgot or didn't know. Is he really a South Korean spy? Is he really a good guy?

As we walked there was a slight breeze and the ospreys were flying over the water searching for fish.

Ospreys look like little eagles with a partially white head, but they are much smaller. There are at least a dozen birds living in this area because the water is shallow which provides good fishing. Ospreys circle over head until they see a small fish; then they dive and pluck the fish right out of the water. Only their talons get wet.

Park stood there looking at them gliding through the air and asked, "Isn't that your national bird, the bald eagle?"

"No, that's an osprey or fish hawk."

"I never saw one before. This is a really nice place here. It's so peaceful."

"Yeah, we like it and wanna keep it that

way."

"These mangroves are very dense and provide excellent cover. My men probably would use them to get up close to your Tocabaga Bridge."

"I agree with that because otherwise they need to swim to the island. Believe me, swimming here is very dangerous because of the sharks."

We finally reached the bridge and Park walked underneath surveying the channel and the underside of the structure. Standing under the bridge in the shade felt good. He looked up at the old rusted metal beams and commented, "It would be almost impossible to climb across this bridge using the super structure."

"I could have told you that. There's no way to cross this channel unless you swim."

Park looked at me and nodded his head in agreement. "You're right. To even get to the bridge is impossible with that 100 meter open area."

Where the mangroves end there is a clear open beach area. It is a natural open space that is about 300 feet long or 100 meters, on both sides of the road. To make it across this open space, to the bridge, without being spotted is impossible.

The main secret, which I didn't tell Park, was the road is lined on both sides with 500

Claymore mines. These mines can be activated by motion detectors or by manual operation. This is why we call it the Road of Death. The Claymore mines could stop any large force in their tracks.

My phone rang and it was from Captain Sessions. I stepped away from Park and answered the phone. Sessions spoke, "Jack, SOCOM checked out Colonel Park, Kang-Dae. His contact at the KIA, General Park, was assassinated a year ago. No one could confirm that Park is a KIA agent. That's all I can tell you."

"Ok, thanks for the information Captain." Hanging up, I thought another FUBAR is going to happen.

Park was sitting under the bridge, in the shade, as I walked up to Mike and Tommy about 50 feet away. I told them, "I got bad news. SOCOM says General Park was killed a year ago. No one at Korea Intelligence can confirm Park and his men are agents."

Mike said, "We'll need to terminate them all."

"I agree with that," Tommy replied.

"What if we let Park sit here on the bridge waiting for his men? We'll use him as bait to get them to surrender," I suggested.

"Surrender? Why do you want dangerous commies running around?"

"I'm not sure they're commies. We need to give them the benefit of the doubt."

Mike said, "Man, you're getting soft."

"I'm not getting soft. I need to be 100 percent sure they're commies. Park did show us the GPS bugs. He knew about Master Yoon, I think. There is only one way to find out if what he told us is true."

"How's that?" Tommy asked.

"I need to talk to Master Yoon, if he's still alive. He'd be about 80 years old by now."

"Do you have his phone number after all these years?"

"I need to check my files. Right now I want both of you to stay with Park and me. We'll go to my house to get Yoon's number."

We stopped at my house and I went inside to find my little black book, which had phone numbers from 30 years ago. After a little digging I found it. I saved the number in my cell phone and walked out the door to find little Johnny talking to Park as they sat on the patio.

Johnny asked, "Why do you have a different uniform? What do the red stars mean? Are you a commie?"

Before Park could answer I said, "Johnny, that's enough questions."

KD replied, "No, its ok. I love kids even if I don't have any of my own. Johnny, I am a South Korean spy. I've been spying on the Red Chinese Army. Now I'm here and I hope to live on Tocabaga in peace." I could tell KD really did like kids as he patted Johnny on the back. Johnny seemed to like Park.

I sat down and told him, "KD, I have bad news for you. General Park at the KIA was killed last year. I'm sorry to give you that news."

KD hung his head, put his hands over his eyes, and didn't speak for a couple of minutes. "Who killed my Father?"

"I don't know, but he was assassinated by someone in the KIA. This means your story can't be verified by him. I have another idea however, and that's to call Master Yoon. If he's still alive he can verify who you really are."

"Ok, please call him."

We sat on my patio for another hour waiting for 6 pm. KD talked to all my grandkids telling them who he was. My wife brought us out some fruit and lemon tea to help pass the time.

I pulled out my phone and said, "Well it's time to call." I dialed the number and the phone rang five times before someone picked it up and I said, "Yŏboseyo, kŏgiga samsamoul sa oich'irimnikka? (Hello, is this 335-4527?)"

"Ye, kŭrŏssŭmnida. (Yes, it is.)" A woman's voice answered.

"Yoon sŭseŭng-nim chom taejuseyo. (May I talk to Master Yoon, please.)"

"Nugushirago halkkayo? (Who's calling please?)"

"Chŏnŭn Jack Gunnjŭimnida. (This is Jack Gunn.)"

"Chamkkanman kidarishipshio. (Just a moment.)"

I heard his old voice, the voice of Master Yoon. "Annyŏnghashimnikka, Gunnjŭ ssi? (How are you Mr. Gunn?)"

I responded in English, "Master Yoon I'm fine. How are you?"

Since the first Korean War in 1950 English is the second language of Korea. All students are required to study English for at least five years. Most people can speak, read, and write English by the time they finish high school.

"I am well, considering my age."

"Master, I'm calling you from my home in Florida. I have an important question."

"How may I help you?"

"Do you remember a student named Park, Kang-Dae?"

"What is his birth sign?"

"He's a Rat."

"Just a moment I will check my records." Five minutes go by and Master Yoon came back on line. "Park, Kang-Dae was my student. He never finished his training because he was called to active military duty. His Father was General Park who was in charge of the KIA. His great-great-grandfather was Park, Chung-Hee, the first duly elected President of South Korea. Why do you ask about him?"

"He's here with me in Florida. I had to verify who he really is."

"Is there anything else Jack Gunn?"

"I have nothing else Master Yoon. I wish you good health and a long life."

"Thank you, Jack Gunn. I wish you the same. Please call more often than once every 20 years. Good-bye." He hung up before I could say good-bye. Master Yoon never liked using the phone. He preferred face-to-face communication.

I sat there as everyone waited for me to advise what Yoon had told me. I sat back, took a sip of tea, looked at Park and told him, "Well, Master Yoon confirmed you were a student and that your father was a General working for the KIA. Your great-great-grandfather was the first duly elected President. You were telling the truth." I stood up and shook his hand. "Welcome to Tocabaga."

Tommy and Mike looked at each other and also shook hands with KD. Everything he told us was true so we had no reason doubt him. KD had dinner with my family and we made him feel at home.

After dinner I suggested that Park retire for the night at the Fort. He could stay in one of the empty officer's quarters. While driving to the Fort I stopped at the security check point and advised the guards that Park would be staying at the Fort. I didn't want the patrols to shoot him by mistake.

Stopping at the quarters I gave him a room key and a radio to contact me if needed. I advised him that he was on his own here for the night. I warned him not to roam around because of the roving security patrols. I handed him a loaded M4 with three extra magazines. Tomorrow we would provide him fatigues with the necessary combat equipment.

Park touched my arm and said, "Thank you

for everything. I swear my loyalty to you and I'll do my best to protect Tocabaga."

"Thank you, KD." I pulled out my Black Bear fighting knife. "There's an old Native American Indian custom that close friends would become blood brothers. I cut the palm of my hand and your hand. Then we hold them together sharing the blood, so to speak."

Park told me. "I've seen this in old American Indian movies."

KD held out his hand; I sliced it open and blood quickly flowed out. I sliced mine and we shook hands tightly holding them together while looking each other in the eye.

"KD, we're now blood brothers forever. This cannot be undone. We promise to protect and help each other as normal brothers would do."

"Jack, I won't let you down." It was kinda weird becoming his blood brother. When I was a little kid we did this all the time, but we aren't kids anymore. I did this ceremony to show KD that I trusted him and that he could trust me. We had just bonded expecting to be life-long blood brothers with each other.

I advised him, "Remember, don't go roaming around in the dark. Stay in your room. I'll pick you up at 7 am sharp." As I drove away KD waved at me.

I stopped at the bar for a nightcap feeling pretty good about the way things turned out today. Arriving home I told my family that KD and I had become blood brothers. No one said a word about it other than my wife, who thought it was a good gesture.

JULY 9, 2025

I woke up to the birds singing and my grandkids yelling. After taking a shower I went to the kitchen and poured a cup of mud. I advise Hemmi to set an extra plate for breakfast because KD would be joining us.

I stepped out on the patio for a smoke only to find Tommy, Ron, and Jim Bo already sitting there. It had rained last night so it was very humid and I started to perspire almost instantly.

I pulled out a smoke and Jim Bo said, "You need to give up that nasty habit." I didn't say a word as I took a deep drag and blew smoke in his direction.

I told my crew, "KD is coming for breakfast and then we need a strategy to locate his men."

"I still don't trust Park," Tommy stated. "Blood brother or not he seems sneaky to me."

I took a sip of coffee and commented. "Park and his men could be a big asset if we have a run in with the commies. It's only a matter of time before they come back with more troops. We need all the fighters we can get. Tommy, let's go pick up KD for breakfast."

We walked into the garage and opened the gun safe. We never go anywhere without our guns and combat gear.

Our truck splashed though puddles left on the road from the rain. Reaching the check point Tommy stopped and asked the guards if everything was ok. They reported there were no problems.

We pulled up to the quarters assigned to Park. I got out and knocked on the door. There was no reply, so I opened the door to the unit and looked inside. No one was there. The AC and lights were turned off.

"Tommy, Park isn't here. I'm going over to the mess hall to look for him."

He wasn't at the mess hall so I pulled out my radio. "Park, come in … Park, come in." There was no reply.

I walked back to the truck and Tommy

rubbed it in. "See, I told you not to trust him."

"Why do you have a hard-on about Park?"

"When I was in Korea, I worked with a South Korean sniper team. One of them turned out to be a traitor. He killed his spotter and tired to kill me. No one suspected that he was a North Korean agent."

"Well, I doubt Park is a double agent. Let's try to find out what happened to him."

Tommy walked over to the door of the housing unit and looked around. "There's no sign of a struggle inside or outside. Here's some tracks. Three people where here."

I bent over and looked at the footprints in the wet grass. Tommy started to follow the tracks which led us to the blacktop parking lot where the footprints disappeared. The tracks indicated they were headed towards the beach.

I said, "Let's go to the beach and see if we can pick up the tracks." We walked to the beach and searched around. The tracks were easy to spot in the pristine sand.

There were three sets of foot prints leading to the edge of the water. On the beach, at the water line, there was a groove in the sand which looked like a small boat had been there. The footprints led right to it.

Tommy stated, "Well there is no doubt that Park left here with two other men by boat. Looking at this groove I'd guess it was a little rubber boat." We scanned the water looking for a boat, but saw none.

"What the hell is Park doing?" I commented.

"Damn if I know, but I told you not to trust him." Tommy rubbed it in again.

"Maybe a couple of his men found him and he went to talk the others into surrendering."

"If so, why didn't he leave a note telling us or give you a shout on the radio?"

"I don't know. Maybe he's in trouble." I really thought Park was in some kind of trouble.

Tommy looked at me and shook his head in a negative way. "Yeah, and maybe he's up to no good. Now he knows the lay-out of the Fort and Tocabaga. Maybe they're planning to attack us."

I scanned the water once again hoping to spot the little boat and my blood brother. I couldn't believe he would do anything to hurt us.

I answered, "Get serious. They wouldn't attack us with sixteen men."

"Maybe not, but if they're working for the

Chinese Army they could pass on the information. They could be spying on us. We need more security on this beach right away. I bet they come back to this very same spot."

Without the Rangers here the only thing we can do is have the Amazon Warriors patrol the beach area. We started to walk back to the housing unit and I took one last look at the water hoping to see a boat.

Reaching the quarters, Tommy said, "Here's my plan. Post our guards along the three mile beach in teams of two every eight hundred yards. Pull six men from the main bridge, and have them be a roving patrol. Put everyone on full alert ready to respond quickly in case of an invasion."

"An invasion by who?"

"An invasion by Park and his men."

"Let me think about it. Let's head back home and get some food."

Heading home I tried to radio Park again just in case his radio was on. "Park, if you can hear me please report at once. If you need help let me know."

"You're wasting your time. He's with his buddies planning how to overthrow Tocabaga," Tommy commented.

We arrived home and Hemmi asked, "Where is Mr. Park?" I told her the bad news and she wasn't surprised. Maybe I am getting too old and soft. After we ate breakfast I set up a meeting with my key people at the bar to discuss our next steps.

In attendance were Rick, Tony, Jim Bo, Tommy, Mike, Maggie, and Amy. I started off the meeting advising everyone that Park had disappeared last night by boat. I continued, "At this point we can't trust Park or his men. We need more security at the Fort covering the beach. I want the Amazon Warriors to provide that security." Nodding their heads, Amy and Maggie looked at me indicating concurrence with this idea.

Amy asked, "How do you want us to position guards on the beach?"

"Park knows that the beach is our weak point so I want the Warriors to do roving patrols using trucks. We need three trucks with two Warriors in each one. I also want four teams, with three Warriors in each team, spread out along the beach as look-outs. Keep out of sight. Everyone keep in contact by radio using channel 34. Park has one of our radios so he might be able to listen in."

Amy inquired, "How'd he get one of our radios?"

"I made a big mistake and gave it to him. Anyway Park got away by boat and Tommy thinks he'll come back by boat to the same area."

"What are we looking for and what do you expect will happen?"

"Good questions. I really have no idea what will happen. I can only tell you we're looking for Park and his men. If Tommy is right they'll try to land on the beach somewhere tonight. I want y'all to radio me the second you see a boat coming ashore. I don't want you to start shooting, unless you have no choice. I wanna see what's going on before we start blasting away at them. I'll have a rapid reaction team set up at the Fort ready to move in to provide support.

"Every man here is on the reaction team. We'll have the two Hummers with machine guns and three SAWs. Any comments?"

Rick spoke up. "Where do you think they're at now?"

"My guess is they're at Egmont Key. That's where I would go if I had a boat. No one lives there so it would be a perfect hide out."

Egmont Key is located at the mouth of Tampa Bay, southwest of Fort Desoto Beach about one mile off shore. The island served as a camp for captured Seminoles at the end of the Third

Seminole War. It was later occupied by the Union Navy during the Civil War. In 1898, as the Spanish-American War loomed, Fort Dade was built on the island and remained active until 1923. The ruins of Fort Dade are all that remains on the 450-acre island. For some reason the island is loaded with big rattlesnakes. No one knows how they came to the island.

There is only one entrance into Tampa Bay and that is the channel that runs between Egmont Key and Fort Desoto. Large ships entering can be spotted miles away from on top of the fort.

Tommy said, "They'll probably try to come ashore when it's dark. Lucky for us there's a full moon tonight."

I advised, "Ok, if nothing else make ready. It's gonna be a long day and night. Oh, be sure you have plenty of water and something to eat. I don't know how long we're going to be on duty."

We checked all our gear, ammo, and supplies putting what we didn't want to carry into the two Hummers. It was 10 am when my rapid reaction team drove to the Fort to set up on top of the highest wall, which was a good forty feet tall. This allowed an unobstructed view in all directions. It's actually not a wall but a big hill of dirt with bushes that cover the water side of the Fort's cement wall. Behind the wall are big old Civil War mortars which are no longer useable.

Two of my men would be on look out and rotate with the other four every two hours. An hour later the Amazon Warriors radioed me that they were all set up and on duty. It was a warm day but there was a nice sea breeze blowing in which helped cool us off.

It was around 5 pm and we hadn't seen anything but birds flying around. I asked Tony to go downtown and round up some food for us and the Warriors. We would take turns eating while keeping up our guard.

Sunset came and the bright orange ball slowly dropped into the water throwing off a brilliant glowing sky mixed with blue, purple, red, and orange. You never get tired of watching a Florida sunset. Each one is beautiful in its own way.

By 9 pm it was dark but there was a full moon rising and soon it would be overhead. The moon glowed, shining off the water, providing us good visibility.

The Fort is isolated and there are many types of animals that come out at night. You don't hear them all the time but every now and then some creature scoots by in the bushes or an owl flies overhead. It's quiet and you can hear the rhythmic waves striking the beach. It's a never-ending noise that blends in and becomes a natural sound. After a while you don't notice the pounding waves.

JULY 10, 2025

AFTER MIDNIGHT

The moon was overhead and it was about 2 am when Tony radioed, "Jack, I hear a motor out there, but I don't see anything."

"I'll be right there." I climbed up the hill and sat down next to Tony and Jim Bo. "Where's the sound coming from?"

Tony pointed and advised me, "Over there, between Egmont and here. It's in the middle of the channel."

I looked with my naked eyes and didn't see any boat, but the water looked disturbed. Something was throwing up a very small wake. I could barely hear a low humming noise coming from the same direction. Picking up my M4 I looked through the night vision FLIR. I could see a faint glow of heat but nothing else. The glow wasn't enough to suggest that there was a boat, but it still made me wonder what the hell it was. It could be coming from Egmont Island.

"Tony look at this." I gave him my M4 to look through the FLIR. "What do you think?" Tony handed the gun to Jim Bo.

"I think there's a boat there that we can't see," Jim Bo said.

"I agree," Tony replied.

"That's what I think also." Then the faint humming stopped so I looked again in that direction with the FLIR and the heat signature was gone.

"It's gone now. Are we cracking up?"

"I don't think so," Tony answered. "We all saw it and heard it."

I got on the radio and told everyone to be alert because something strange was going on. We heard something and spotted a weak heat source in the channel, but we couldn't identify what it was.

I thought maybe it's a submarine of some kind. Yeah that's gotta be a sub out there. The situation was very spooky. I radioed the Warriors to pull back to the shark channel bridge and set up a defensive position there. Something didn't feel right. My sixth sense told me something was going to pop out of the water and surprise us.

Amy radioed, "Ok, we're all back at the bridge. What now?"

I replied, "Spread out and make a defensive line on the north side of the bridge. Just wait there for further orders."

I sat on the hill scanning the water. My intuition and combat experience told me that we were in danger. Then the humming sound came back and I saw a ripple in the water. A small wake rolled across an otherwise smooth flat surface. If it weren't for the full moon I wouldn't have seen the water turning over making a small white cap which quickly disappeared.

I thought the wave was about a half mile away and the M2 machine guns can reach that far. I told my men, "Tony, Jim Bo, bring the Hummers to the beach and start shooting those machine guns toward that noise. Let's see if the rounds hit anything."

"Shoot at what? There is nothing there," Tony said.

"Just shoot about 30 feet above the water line. Spray bullets all over the place."

"Ok, we're on the way."

I sat on the hilltop watching the trucks pull onto the beach. Tommy walked up behind me and scared the shit out of me as the machine guns were spitting fire at an unseen target.

Tommy yelled over the noise, "Look, the tracers are just disappearing into thin air." You couldn't tell if the bullets where hitting anything. After about 30 rounds from each gun they stopped firing.

"Well Boss, did you see anything?" Jim Bo asked, over the radio.

"Negative, Jim Bo. Come on back."

Just then I heard a whistle, the sound of an incoming cannon round. KABOOM … the round looked like it made a direct hit on the truck Tony was driving. The heavy Humvee flipped over on its side. More rounds followed hitting the beach one by one, as if in slow motion, making a trail up the hill to my location.

Tony appeared to be ok because I saw him scramble out of his truck and jump into the other one with Jim Bo. They sped away from the cannon fire.

I shouted to Tommy, "Let's get the hell out of here."

I peered out into the night with my FLIR, but couldn't see any hint of a heat source. We rolled down the hill out of the line of fire and ducked behind the cement jail cell, since it was totally bomb proof.

Rounds were falling all over the area. Jim Bo pulled up stopping a few feet away and yelled, "Let's go!" The six of us squeezed into the Hummer and roared away as flying debris from the exploding rounds bounced off the vehicle.

I asked, "Tony, you ok?"

"Yeah, just some minor cuts and a big headache."

We were on the main road out of range and Jim Bo stopped the truck when he heard my radio crackle, "Jack, come in. This is Colonel Park." We all looked at each other in disbelief. "Jack, you're being invaded. Get off the beach now. Meet me at the camp ground building and I'll fill you in."

Jim Bo asked, "What do you wanna do?"

Tommy warned me, "It's a trap, don't trust him."

"We have no choice. Drive to the camp ground," I ordered. "Tommy you man the fifty just in case it's a trap."

I clicked the radio, "Park, we're on the

way."

We had no sooner started to move and … KABOOM … a big explosion rocked the Hummer shaking us up. I hit my head on the side of the truck. Lucky for us the old Hummer was still running. Jim Bo floored it to get us out of the line of fire.

Dazed, with blood running down my face, I yelled, "What the hell hit us?"

"I think it was an RPG," Tommy replied.

"Who the hell is shooting at us?" As we pulled away I could hear bullets hitting our truck.

"I don't know I can't see anyone," Jim Bo replied. Our truck was getting pelted by automatic rifle fire, but we couldn't see anyone shooting at us. We quickly pulled away and made it to the camp ground office which is about a mile down the road.

I dismounted and looked around for Colonel Park, but he wasn't there. I called out, "Park, where are you?" I opened the door to the small office building and peeked inside.

I shouted to everyone, "There's no one here!"

Tommy, sitting in the machine gun turret, yelled, "See, I told you it was a trap!" I heard him rack the big 50 caliber machine gun.

I thought, oh no, more FUBAR!

That's all for now.

GOD BLESS AMERICA, LAND OF THE FREE, AND HOME OF THE BRAVE!

Jack Gunn

PS: Read my article on Gun Selection. It gives advice to first-time gun buyers; how to choose the correct gun for defense or hunting.

THOMAS H. WARD

GUN SELECTION

This article will cover gun selection based on what is the most popular ammunition. The gun is your most important asset. Without ammunition, however, your gun is worthless. What kind of guns should one own? Based on my 40 years of gun experience the type of gun and caliber is very important for your protection. Guns have only two main purposes which are hunting and self protection. Of course, any of the guns mentioned in this article can be used for hunting as well as self defense. The question is which gun is the best tool for the job.

For people new to guns I try to explain the differences in a simple manner. When purchasing your first gun it is a confusing matter to choose the correct gun with the large selection in the market. I have had many people ask me, what type of gun should I purchase? Where do you go to learn to shoot?

GUNS FOR HUNTING

The most popular ammunition is the .22 long round and the 12 gauge shotgun round. This ammo is easy to obtain and that is what is important. The more popular the ammo is the easier it is to find when you run out of ammunition.

I break down guns into two categories which are hunting guns and tactical guns or combat weapons. There may come a time when you will need to hunt for food. There are two types of hunting guns that can dispatch most animals and that is a 12 gauge shotgun and a .22 caliber rifle or pistol. These two guns allow you good flexibility. The shotgun you can use bird shot for hunting birds or rabbits and slugs for hunting deer or larger animals. In addition a 12 gauge with slugs or buck shot is a great weapon to use for protection at close range.

The one drawback is that shotgun shells are expensive and heavy to carry and too large to store many of them. Shotguns come mostly in semi-automatic and pump type. They hold 5 to 8 rounds. The difference is the semi-auto you just load and pull the trigger. The faster you pull the trigger the faster it shoots. The pump needs to be pumped or cocked each time to shoot it. I prefer the semi-auto type because it is faster, easier to clean and use. Double barrel or single shot shotguns are not worth owning since you have to reload every time you fire it.

Do not under estimate the .22 rifle or long barrel pistol as it can be used on birds and or small rodents as well as be a tool for self defense. A .22 with hollow point bullets is an easy weapon to use and you can carry a lot of ammunition since the bullets are so small. You can store 5,000 rounds of this ammo in a desk due to its small size. A .22 rifle has a 200 yard range and 6 inch barrel pistol has a 50 yard range.

The 12 gauge shotgun and a .22caliber rifle are a must to own. A .22 rifle also comes in pump or semi-auto types. The choice is up to you. As for 22 pistols there is only one that I will mention and that is the Ruger target model as it is the best you can buy.

My selection for a shotgun is a Remington semi-auto model that handles 2 ¾ inch shells. Purchase a shotgun that has a stock and forearm that is made of modern plastic as it can stand up better to the elements.

GUNS FOR SELF DEFENSE

There are many types of combat pistol and rifle ammunition. The selection of the ammunition is critical to the type of combat rifle or combat pistol you will select for protection. The shotgun and .22 rifle mentioned above are dual purpose weapons but are mainly for hunting. The pistols and rifles mentioned below are really the weapons you need for total protection. These are guns that contain high capacity magazines.

What other types of guns do you need to

survive? Well let us first look at what is the most popular type of ammunition used to make our selection. Having enough ammo will be your biggest problem. The fact is most police and military handguns are 9 mm. The 45 caliber and 40 calibers are also popular but not as common as 9mm luger ammo. The 9mm ammo is also less expensive to purchase.

For rifles there are only three major types of calibers that are widely used by the police and military. One is the .223 Winchester also known as the 5.56mm NATO round. The other is the AK 47 round 7.62 x39, a round used by the military and some police around the world. This is the most popular ammo used by terrorists and gangs because the AK 47 is an inexpensive weapon or rifle. The last is the .308 Winchester round or 7.62x51 NATO.

The .223 ammo is used by the famous Colt AR15 or the M16 which is now named the M4 carbine, widely used by our military. There are many different manufactures of the so called AR15 design. Some of these AR designs also shoot 7.62x51 NATO which is the basically the same as the .308 Winchester and are called AR10 rifles.

The 7.62x39 and 7.62x51 are not to be confused as they are totally different rounds. The drawback of the 7.62x51round is the cost is higher than the .223 and when you are hauling around 300 rounds they are also heavier. The 7.62 x 51 is a long range round and can exceed 800 yards. The .223 round has an effective range of up to 500 yards.

You can also purchase an AR type rifle that will fire the AK 47 7.62x39mm round. Bushmaster is one of the best manufactures for AR type designs which can be purchased in many different calibers. Several companies also make a .22 caliber AR rifle such as Colt and the Smith and Wesson M&P 15-22.

The most popular type ammunition for a pistol is the 9mm luger round. The most common type for a rifle is the .223 Winchester, also known as the 5.56mmNATO round. Knowing this we can select a number of different pistols, rifles, or carbines to use. For this selection we need to keep in mind durability, ease of cleaning, interchangeability, and ease of use by men or women.

Knowing that we want a handgun that shoots 9mm luger rounds you can note that all 9mm are semi-auto design and are not revolvers. Semi-auto means it has a magazine that holds the bullets and some can hold up to 18 rounds before reloading. There are two handguns that I recommend which are a Glock and a Springfield Armory model XD. I own both and they are the best dependable handguns on the market. This is not to say there are not other good brands but based on my shooting experience buying one of these handguns you cannot go wrong.

My favorite is the Glock Model 17 because it is dependable and very easy to clean and repair. Yes, sometimes guns break so you should have some extra parts or a backup gun or two if possible. Each gun comes with an assembly manual and the Glock can be taken apart by just removing the slide and one pin which is pushed out. I have shot thousands of rounds and only had my Glock break one time. The trigger return spring broke and I replaced it in 10 minutes with a new one. It is so simple that anyone can work on it. The Glock can be dropped in the mud, run over by a truck and still shoot. It can be fired under water and the barrel life is 350,000 rounds which is more than you will ever shoot in your life time.

Basically all AR15 type rifles are the same design and are easy to take apart for cleaning. The models may have different names from different manufactures such as Armalite SPR Mod 1 which is basically the same as a Colt CAR15 or carbine model of the AR 15 rifle.

It pays to buy a good quality rifle from a well known manufacturer even if it may cost a little more. Remember your life may depend on this weapon. If you buy an AR type rifle then find out what parts you may need to replace by asking the manufacture. I recommend buying two weapons of the same type this way you have a back up and you do not have to learn about different weapons and the assemblies. Parts between different manufactures' are not necessarily interchangeable. The AR15 can be cleaned in about 10 minutes just by pushing out a pin which opens the rifle up. It is also light weight so men and women can use it. The recoil is very low which is important for accurate firing. I recommend the Colt brand AR15 .223 as this is a dependable weapon which has been on the market many years.

Some manufactures such as Colt have also made CAR15 carbines that use the pistol 9mm luger round. This is an excellent weapon that has very little recoil but has a limited range of about 100 yards. It is made for close quarter combat situations. Having a CAR15 9mm is a good choice since you can use the same ammo as your 9mm handgun.

To summarize the guns needed are; a 12 gauge shotgun semi-automatic type, a .22 rifle or target pistol, a 9mm luger Glock handgun, and a .223 (5.56 NATO) AR15 design rifle or a CAR15 9mm carbine. I would choose to have two guns of each type so you have a backup. How much ammo do you need? It is up to you to decide, but the more the better as the gun is worthless without ammunition. If you can only own one or two guns then the AR15 rifle and the 9mm Glock are my choices.

Everyone in your family should know how to shoot each type of gun. I suggest one gun for each family member. Gun selection should be made by what each member of the family likes best to shoot. One may like a .22 caliber and one may like a 9mm Glock. Remember your family is also your Army to help protect each other. So proper training is very important. Do not spare any expense on training. Do not buy cheap unreliable guns.

GUN SAFETY

If you have no experience with guns then it is suggested that you learn by going to your local gun store or shooting range and take lessons from a good instructor. If you have a friend who shoots go with him to the range. The National Rifle Association or NRA is a valuable resource to use for this learning process.

NRA has safety rules which you can find listed on line. The worst thing you can do is buy a gun and not know how to use it or even load it. If you are faced with a threat to your life or that of your family then you better know how to use the weapon with some degree of skill. The more skillful you are the better your chance of survival will be.

We are talking life and death situations that require split second decisions on your part so shooting practice is a very necessary. Join a local shooting club.

I stress do not buy a gun just to have one. Do not buy a gun if you will never practice or shoot it. How much practice do you need? Based on my experience I think shooting your weapon at least one to two hours per week is necessary to become a good shot and learn to know everything about your gun. I know many people who shoot two hours a week. I also stress go take combat shooting lessons at a gun school such as Gun Sight or Front Sight. They will train you in Home Defense, Vehicle Defense, Tactical Rifle, Pistol, and Shotgun use. Be the best you can be as learning to shoot is more than just going to the range and pulling the trigger.

Above all be a safe shooter and follow the safety rules. When not in use keep you guns locked up so kids cannot access them and they cannot be stolen from you. I strongly suggest a gun safe to store your guns and ammo as it will give you peace of mind. You can also keep other valuables in the safe. Shooting can be a great hobby providing much enjoyment and fun for the whole family. Shoot safe and shoot straight.

THOMAS H. WARD

DRAMATIS PERSONAE

Albert Madison – Navy Vet. who comes to Tocabaga with wife and two kids

Barry – A quisling killed by the Gunn family

Billy – Kid found living on the street with his sister Rosie and brother Peter

Brogan – A Tocabaga security guard who went MIA

Bok Lam – A Chinese man and close friend of Jack's since high school

Buck – Motorcycle gang leader killed by Maggie

Chase – A quisling

Colonel Turner – Commanding Officer of the Army Rangers based at Fort Desoto

Colonel Park - aka Captain Kim a South Korean spy

Corporal Phillips – In charge of the communications office at Fort Desoto

Captain Sessions – Combat officer, commands and controls combat operations in the field

Captain Riley – Female tank commander, girl friend of Captain Sessions

Captain Zhu Lei – A commie killed by Tommy

Chris – Tocabaga security guard and close friend of Jack

Dew – A quisling killed by the Gunn family

Dr. Carl Urban – The inventor of the RCCD Units and friend of Jack's

Dr. Carl Urban, Jr. – Son of Dr. Urban

Dr. Alvin Sinclair – Robot inventor and Commie killed by Jack

Ellen – A lonely woman

First Lt. Fisher – TALOS Warrior, Platoon commander

Farmer John – An old farmer saved by Jack, now living on Tocabaga

Guy Allen or GA – Suspected spy living on Tocabaga was killed by Jack

General Chen – A Red Chinese Army General in charge of the Florida invasion force

General Harper – Commander of the Rangers located at SOCOM

George Taylor – A nice kid who was bullied in school by Nick

Hemmi – Wife of Jack Gunn

Joe – RCCD tech. Supervisor; a tough guy killed by

Jack

Little Johnny – Adopted grandson of Jack's

Johnny the Fisherman – A quisling killed by security

Jill – A warrior killed by Feds

Jim Bo – Husband to Amy and son-in-law of Jack

Jimmy Smith – A bully from years ago

Ken – US Deputy Marshal who went missing

Leroy – The man who killed Jack's little brother Mike

Mike – Jack Gunn's little brother killed by a doper

Maggie – Wife of Robbie, who is in charge of the farming

Mr. Johnson or Famer John – Old time Farmer

Mr. Horn – Pig farmer and dirtbag who wanted to kidnap Maggie for breeding

Nick – A bully from Junior High School

Peter – Little nine year old brother to Rosie

Rosie – A fifteen year old girl Jack found living on the street

Robbie – Best friend of Jack Gunn, a Tocabaga security guard killed by the FPF on April 27, 2025

Ron – Brother of Jack Gunn Retired Navy vet. Part

of Tocabaga security.

Rick – President of Tocabaga Association, security team member

Sally – A warrior killed by Feds

Scotty – A quisling killed by security

Sergeant Hammer – Army Ranger

Sergeant First Class Dale – killed in action

Sergeant Major Willis – Ranger squad leader and security guard for Jack

Sergeant Cain – the Drone Master

Sergeant Smith - Army Ranger assigned as security guard for Jack

Stan – Deputy Marshal

Sue – Wife of Albert Madison

Tommy Gunn – Son of Jack Gunn and a retired Marine Scout Sniper

Tony – Bar keeper and sharp-shooter for Tocabaga security

Trini – Amazon Warrior who killed Troy

Troy – A quisling killed by security

Victor Elway – An old farmer from Ellenton now living on Tocabaga with his friend Farmer John

Zack – A quisling killed by the Gunn family

OTHER BOOKS BY THOMAS H. WARD

THE TOCABAGA CHRONICLES:

TOCABAGA 1: Revised Edition

TOCABAGA 2: Theoterrorism

TOCABAGA 3: Warm Blood – Cold Steel

TOCABAGA 4: The Talos Warriors

TOCABAGA 5: The Quislings & Androktones

TOCABAGA 6: The Dimachaerus Clan - Missing In Action

TOCABAGA 7: Pàn Guó Zuì - High Treason

TOCABAGA 8: The Invisibles

CONTACT THOMAS H. WARD:

Website: www.ThomasHWardBooks.com
Email: Tocabaga.Jack@gmail.com
Facebook: www.Facebook.com/Tocabaga